I0645447

THE GHOST OF

MILE **43**

CRAIG RODGERS

Death of Print

Cover and book design by Alan Good

Originally published by Soft Cartel. Second edition published 2021 by Death of Print

Deathofprint.press

Print ISBN: 978-0-9981710-3-6
Ebook ISBN: 9781087941271

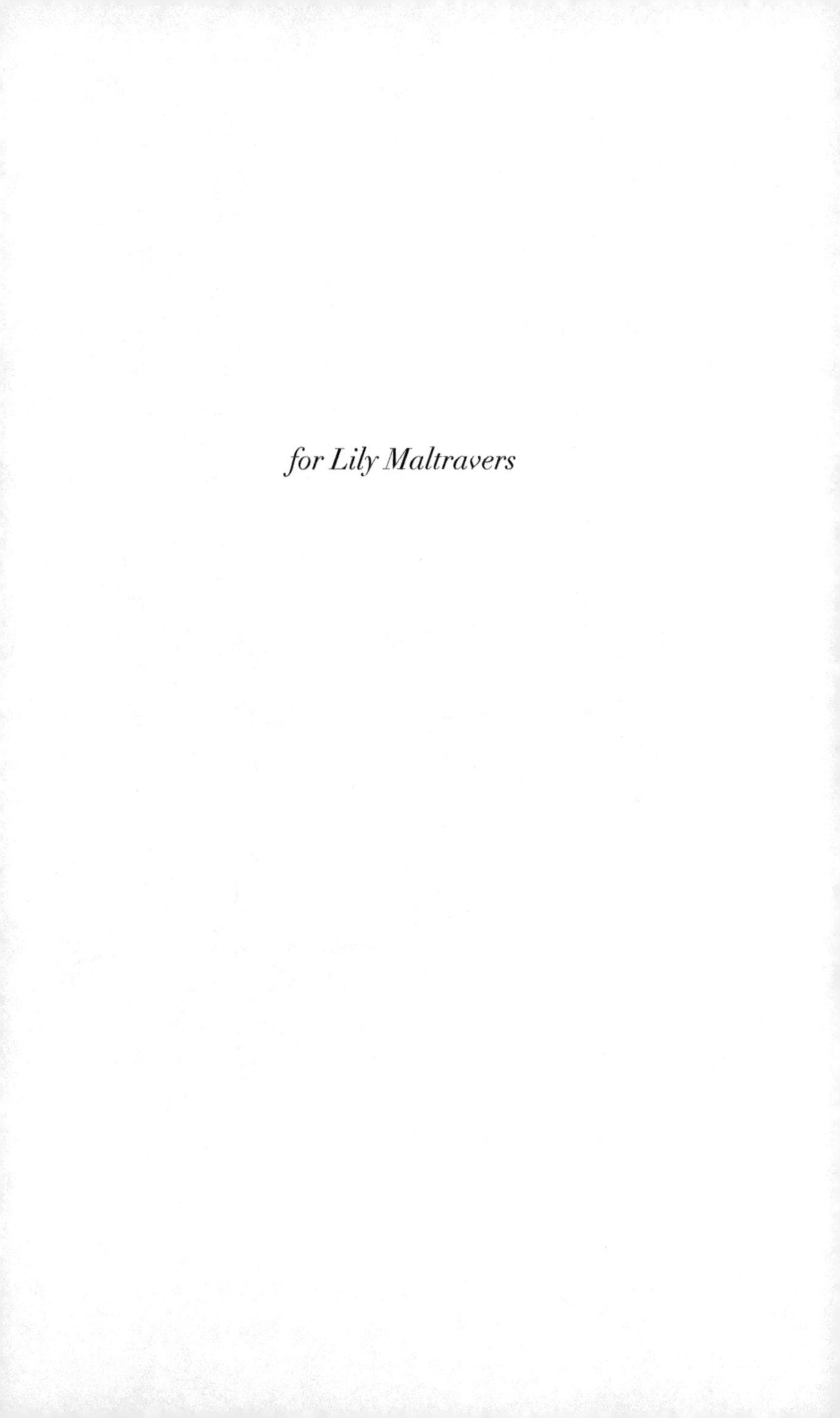

for Lily Maltravers

1

His lawyer isn't coming. He pretends to make a call and he pretends his call goes unanswered but he knows his lawyer won't pick up. He makes them wait; the banker, the banker's counsel. He shrugs, he says there must be some delay. The banker checks a watch and asks him to call again but he says just wait, just wait.

Papers sit on the coffee table. A pen is laid across their top. He stares at the pages, unblinking for long minutes.

"Any objection to me smoking?"

The banker scoffs.

"I do. In here? Yeah I do."

"It's my house."

"It isn't."

He does not respond. He sits staring at the stack of paperwork and then he is standing, he is loosening and removing a tie which he lays across the table and he is taking things from his pockets of pants and jacket; a business card, the phone, a ring of keys.

"I'm gonna smoke outside."

He takes up a green plastic lighter and he moves to the door and out and it is only after the exile is gone that the banker and the banker's counsel take notice of the pack of cigarettes left behind with the rest.

The driveway is a concrete slope leaning hard toward the street. The exile is standing at the top with hands in pants pockets when the banker's counsel comes out to find him. The exile isn't smoking. He isn't doing anything. The counsel stands by in the quiet and seconds fall away and then the exile is pulling hand from pocket and he is shaking a wrist, he is looking at his watch. The counsel speaks up.

"You need to get back to work?"

"I guess I don't."

The counsel looks down and the exile looks out at the street and there is a moment when nothing is said, when something is waiting to be said, and then it is there, the counsel is saying fighting it isn't worth the trouble, not now when it's already done, and he waits for some reply that doesn't come, he waits thirty seconds or he waits a full minute before again going into the house.

The street is lined with house after house, not all alike but each poured whole from four or five variations. A voice speaks somewhere nearby behind window or wall and some blocks away the hushed passage of traffic unseen goes on its way. Here life exists in its static hum as players in a thousand dramas put on their own private shows. The exile looks around at this street and this world and he takes a step, and another, and another, and when he reaches the street he keeps going.

***

A bell sounds as he enters, electronic and unreal. He nods at a clerk behind the counter. The shelves between which the exile meanders are filled with jars and bottles and baubles in wrappers; candy, soda, motor oil. He takes up a snack bar all caramel and salt and he continues his browsing. At the coolers he halts. He opens a glass

9

door and goes on looking. Door glosses over. In time he takes out a water.

He lays items on the counter. The clerk types numbers into a register and leans in to see what has just been typed and then the clerk types again. The exile watches the clerk do these things and he eyes racks of blue and red and tan boxes stacked in rows at the clerk's back.

"Your total."

The clerk turns a readout around to face the exile, and a wallet is coming out, and money is taken in folds from wallet pocket, small bills, large bills, hundreds. He sets a five on the counter and beside it he lays the wallet. The fold of bills he keeps, he shoves in a wad into a jacket pocket. The clerk is counting out change and when he tells the clerk to keep it the clerk goes on counting.

Outside a man lurks squatting on stoop. When a gray sedan stops at a pump to get gas the man stands and he approaches the motorist, and he's pointing, he's gesturing. A car out of gas, a few dollars needed. The motorist knows this grift and she turns the grifter away. The exile looks on.

The clerk has finished the count. Coins and bills are passed across and the exile is taking them and shoving them into one pocket even as he's taking another five from inside his jacket. Again he lays money on the counter.

"All right, thanks."

The clerk puts the five in a hip pocket of jeans. The exile again turns to watch the motorist. A stranger in a smart suit jacket, business skirt. The exile asks the clerk what her bill comes to and when he is told he pays that too. He goes outside with a paper sack containing the items he's bought.

The motorist is looking into a leather bag and sorting through items it holds. She looks up at the exile's approach. He smiles, he waves. He asks if she can give him a ride to the bus depot. He says he can pay. She looks at him and then past him. She moves on by and pulls open the convenience store door to the ringing of that unreal bell.

The grifter is smoking at his place on the stoop.

"She wasn't buying, huh. I already tried."

The exile points at the hand holding the cigarette.

"Can I get one of those?"

The grifter looks at his own hand. He looks at the exile and he squints. He does not respond but only takes a pack from a pocket and shakes one out for the exile to take. He pulls it from the pack and he lights it with his plastic lighter. He lowers himself to the pavement. Smoke drifts from lips. In the street beyond the pumps the afternoon traffic begins to congeal as schools let out, jobs let out, institutions empty of their subjects all at once. A car honks and brakes squeal. The exile smokes. He turns. In the convenience store the motorist looks back at him as the clerk is talking. He turns back to the pumps and the street and the world. He smokes. The grifter is talking but the exile is not listening. A bell chimes. The motorist lays a hand on the exile's shoulder.

"Come on."

The exile hands the cigarette off to the grifter and he stands and dusts off the seat of his pants. He takes his purchases and follows the motorist to her car. She gets in and there is a click of a door unlocking and he gets in too. The engine turns over. There comes a dulcet murmur of life returning to this space and then the radio is on and a song is playing. Guitar strumming and brush drum patter. The sound comes on loud and the motorist turns a knob and the sound comes down. She looks at the exile but he is looking out his window. She puts the car in gear.

Traffic starts and stops like waves lapping. The car joins that motion, becomes a part of it. They flow along for blocks and they cut right and they're taking an on-ramp, they're getting onto the interstate where again that trickling progress takes hold. The song ends and then another and then there is a voice that speaks in a lulling cadence about songs already played and other songs to come. The motorist turns the knob and sound recedes to faint chirping. She asks the exile what he does and he says to her he's transitioning, that he's only just left a position, that he's starting over in a way. She's nodding, she's saying she knows how that goes. She says she thinks about doing the same thing. He goes on looking out his window at the slow passage of the world.

"What about you?"

"What?"

"What do you do?"

She tells him. She talks of an office job, a mid-level executive post at a company he's never heard of. She talks of an assistant she doesn't like and of an interning researcher she does. She says the researcher will replace the assistant any day. A moment later she says it again. Any day.

The stops overcome the starts. Traffic slows and it stops and it does not move again. The motorist curses and she looks in the mirror at the miles of cars unmoving behind. She turns the radio back up and runs the dial until it lands on talk. She looks at the radio as she listens. Nothing moves.

The exile is not listening to the motorist lament the things that voice has to say. He looks out at the now-stilled world and he digs a hand into his own thigh. He waits. A foot taps in place. The motorist is saying it's never this bad. She's saying they could walk it faster. Then the exile is unbuckling his seatbelt, he's opening his door.

"Hey."

She gets out only that word and then he is out and he is walking and the world is moving again. He breathes air thick with exhaust and heat but he takes it in with deep lungfuls that he holds onto for moments before letting each go. At times he walks with eyes closed, following only the crunch of gravel underfoot, songs or talk from open car windows, each a distinct universe with its own sounds and smells and lives. Drivers and passengers shout things; words, noises. Some whistle or talk. The exile goes on. Under a bridge he climbs a steep incline to a concrete abutment where he sits with back against the hard surface. He unrolls his paper bag and removes the candy and he peels back the wrapper. Traffic moves and stops. He eats in small bites and drinks from his water and watches the minute changes in what lies before him, the cars, the faces, new ones replacing old in a timescale beholden to none.

Off to his left, a cough and a huff. He turns and there is a man coming down from the road above. The man walks with head turned down and a blanket pulled around him, obscuring his form. He looks up and sees the exile and nods. He approaches, he sits. Another huff, almost a sigh. The exile puts his empty candy wrapper in the paper sack and folds the sack and he puts it in a jacket pocket.

"You're gonna get cold."

The exile turns to look at the transient. A hand protrudes from the transient's wrap. He waves a finger in the exile's direction.

"That jacket. No, man. Nights, it gets cold. You got to get yourself a blanket."

"Well. I'll add it to the list."

"The list. What list? Need a poncho? Need a pillow? A blanket answers all your questions. Need a thing you can lay all your shit on, roll it up, carry it around like a bag? On and on. There's a reason safety blankets are a thing. First concept of home outside the womb is a blanket."

"Did you think that up?"

"Yeah I did. Yeah. A man's got to have a philosophy of life, or else what's he even doing?"

The exile nods. He drinks his water. Cars move in spurts, the motorist in her gray sedan among them, passing by just as any other. The transient is talking, he is asking the exile his name. The exile offers a hand and he says his name is Shaw, and maybe it is.

***

He wakes in the night on a concrete slab. He opens his eyes but there is only black. He closes them, he opens them. Somewhere there is the sound of violence, fist smacking meat, fumbled words begging. A car passes on the interstate below but headlights reveal nothing in their ephemeral passing. Shaw turns. There is an ember in the dark and the whiff of cigarette. The ember moves. Shaw closes his eyes and sleep takes him once more.

16

2

The morning is a gossamer film into which he steps, sliding off a concrete shelf and finding his footing in the shaded underpass where on each side there grows a sheet of diaphanous blue world. Traffic rushes by as a thing unbroken, a solid figure screaming ever onward at speed. His pace mirrors that roaring, raging organism for minutes and then he is veering off and he is climbing a hill to the roadway above. Streets intersect, ramps coming and going, veins leading off to all possible destinations. Shaw waits as cars pass along this ancillary course. Narrow gaps appear but it is not enough. He leans back in search of the end of this impasse. Time goes on. When a break comes he walks with brisk and determined steps across two lanes of access road and then an exit lane and a sidewalk and a grassy patch planted awkward and alien among macadam in every direction and beyond this an open lot lined but empty save for cars left parked in outermost slots, morning workers already arrived or overnight clerks not yet gone.

Glass doors open at his approach. He steps through a foyer filled with the mechanical hum of fans and through a separate set of doors into a warehouse of goods, all manners of things, public donations, retail overstock, shelves lined in places with items arranged and organized at one end and garbage bags piled at another, their contents unsorted, ambiguous treasures. Shaw walks among the stacks and rows, taking up a shoebox and removing its lid. He sets it back and examines another. He opens box after box until he finds a pair of sneakers in his size. He turns the shoebox around and over but there is no tag, no price. He looks left, looks right.

The aisle goes on forever but he is alone here. Someone somewhere is speaking but it is a distant voice, a thing without meaning. Shaw walks the length of the aisle and rounds a corner and walks along another.

A man in a green apron waits in the distance. Unmoving, this apparition. The man in the apron is bent at the waist, hands clasped at his back. He stares at some item there on a shelf and he is staring still as Shaw approaches.

"This doesn't have a tag."

The apron man straightens and he groans. He takes the box and turns it in his hands. He looks at Shaw.

"Make me an offer."

Shaw looks at the box. Seconds go by. That voice in the distance goes on, words unshaped offering up some formless recitation, some arcane litany. Another soon joins or it has been there all along, echoing in the cavernous storehouse of miscellany. Shaw raises a hand. He pulls back a sleeve to show the watch worn there.

"How far will this get me?"

"That watch. That watch will get you a lot of shoes."

"I just need the two."

Pause.

"And a blanket."

The apron man's eyes narrow. He does not look away from the watch as he speaks.

"I can get you a blanket, sure."

The apron man rocks on his feet and he turns and walks along the aisle to the end. Shaw follows at some distance, around an endcap stocked with soaps and shampoos, past others of much the same, down another aisle filled with pillows and linens and all manner of bedding. The apron man stops among these things. He spreads his arms with hands palm up.

"What's your pleasure?"

Shaw walks along the aisle, touching cloth, at times lifting items, measuring weight and feel. He takes up a wool throw patterned in a chaotic paisley of reds and greens and golds. He holds it out for the apron man to appraise and he gives a quick nod of unspoken question. The apron man nods back and he speaks a single word.

"Okay."

Shaw unclasps the watch and slides it from his wrist. He hands it over and he takes his shoes and wool blanket, and without receipt and without shopping bag he does leave this place behind.

***

On the other side of a pane of glass a chalkboard lists line by line a procession of possible futures,

20

cities far flung, names of settings in stories, the ideas of places. On a far wall beyond the window and beyond the milling throng waiting for a bus to arrive or for a friend or loved one to take them away there is a digital board listing much the same index. Sometimes a name will disappear, as if a city has in a blink ceased to be.

Shaw stands outside the bus station looking in for some minutes. He keeps his bundled possessions held to his chest. His eyes run along each of those names, waiting for some inspiration or enlightenment to come from this patient reverie. He gives the effort long minutes but no enlightenment comes.

A city block of blacktop sits beside the station and a gravel lot extends beyond that. Brakes squeal and huff and a bus in the lot releases waves of travelers into the life they'll find here.

Shaw drifts west into the lot and through the stream of wandering bodies to a truck parked along the outskirts. A shutter running along the truck's side is propped open above a counter and a man leans his hands on this counter looking out from that open bay. He moves his lips as Shaw comes near but if there are words there Shaw does not hear. He sets his possessions on the counter.

The man leans down. A ripple of scar comes up out of his shirt and runs along one side of his neck to disappear in his collar. He speaks again and there are words there, a string of syllables whispered. The whispering man asks Shaw what he'll have and Shaw looks over a laminated menu attached to the counter with a length of wire. Po boys, burgers, colas, juices. Shaw taps a finger on a picture and the whispering man brings him a sandwich from a cooler. He lays the sandwich on the counter and he writes out a ticket by hand.

"Drink?"

Shaw says he'll take a water and the man says sure thing and he goes to the same cooler as before. He stands at the open cooler door a moment, as if he has forgotten what his search is for, as if his battery has run down. Then he is taking up a bottle of spring water and closing the cooler and in two long steps he is back at the counter. He takes a plastic bag from a stack of them and he shakes it open and loads in sandwich and water both. Again he writes on the ticket. He speaks his whispers without looking up.

"Anything else?"

Shaw lays a few bills on the counter and he thanks the whispering man. The man knocks a fist on the counter and he holds up one finger. He goes away and comes back and he holds out a plastic bag like the first but larger, sturdier. He nods, he points at the counter where the shoebox sits with the blanket on top, still folded tight.

"For your things."

Shaw thanks the whispering man again. The man waves this off and he is already stepping away from the counter and taking a knife in hand to chop some unseen something on a cutting board there, the satisfying thump of each cut a sort of talk all its own. Shaw watches this. Hypnotic, relaxing, that chopping the sound of the everyday.

He turns to look at the lot at his back. Another bus is loosing its charges into the lot. He gathers his things and puts them into the oversized bag and last of all he places the smaller sack with the sandwich and water in the larger bag with the rest.

There is a flow to their movements. As bodies disembark from each arriving bus they break from a swell of humanity into streams heading off to street, to gravel lot, to station. Shaw with his things moves along with the station current, passing through wide open doors and into an expanse of room lit in warm yellow. The ever present sigh of the open day is left outside, replaced by a wordless hum of some dozens of voices in various stages of use. He moves among the bodies and the noise, seeking a wall and seeking a bench and sitting. He takes and unwraps his sandwich and he eats in small bites. He watches the room.

Two men sit on a bench and another stands at its front and each man holds up a few cards. The standing man lays a card down and one of the sitting men laughs. The laughing man wears a coat too long for his small frame. Fabric the color of mud. The color of brick at night. The standing man lays down all the cards in his hand and so do the others. He takes something from a pocket and hands it over. He says something to the seated men and he turns and walks away.

Shaw watches the game as he eats. When he's done he folds the wax paper in which his sandwich was wrapped and slides it into a pocket, ignorant of the trash bin next to which his bench is set. He takes the bag of his things and lays it beside him on the bench and he pulls the mouth through his fist to form a length of slack that he loops around his wrist and ties once, and with this done he closes his eyes.

Pale light exists on the other side of every window.
He wakes in full night but flood lamps hold back
the dark. The station in its tallow gloom has
emptied of its loitering masses save the occasional
stalwart reading a paperback or sleeping on a
bench as they wait for a bus or a ride or some
event only they can know. Of these few there
remain the gamblers, the laughing man, another
man. The second man has the face of a child,
pink, round, but his hair is thin and graying. The
coat worn before by the laughing man now sits in
a heap at the babyfaced man's back. Shaw rises
and he approaches the bench where their game
goes on.

Cards are shuffled and bridged and dealt. Shaw
watches their game for hand after hand. When he
thinks he knows the rules he asks if he can play.
The laughing man deals him in and the game goes
on. On some hands they bet, on some they do not.
They talk as they play, of plans, of intentions, of
hopes. The babyfaced man is going to hitchhike
from here, he's going to see the country. The
laughing man is going home. They bet cash or
possessions or promises. The game goes on. Each
man loses things and wins things both. When the
game comes to its end the new shoes are lost to

Shaw but as he walks from the station and into the night he does so wrapped in a mud-colored coat.

The food truck is still in the lot. Its frame sits in shadow at the edge of the flood lamp's reach. The shutter is down and there is no light inside, but the tinny brush of music can only just be heard. Shaw knocks on a window. He peers into the cab but no one is there. A light comes on, showing a partition dividing kitchen from cab. The partition slides open and the whispering man ducks from the kitchen into the cab. He stares out at Shaw for some seconds. Then he is rolling down the window. Shaw speaks to the man.

"Do you have anything left from today?"

The whispering man tells Shaw he always has pre-made items that go unsold. He says that they'll be discounted in the morning. He says they always go fast.

Shaw twists a band of white gold on his ring finger. He removes this and holds it up.

"What can I get for this?"

The whispering man takes the ring and he turns it in his hand. He looks it over and he nods. He holds up a finger and gestures back at the shuttered kitchen. He goes that way and so does Shaw.

A minute passes, and another, and another. In time there is a click and a mechanical ratcheting and the shutter opens and the whispering man is there with a sack stuffed with sandwiches and snack cakes and water and more. Shaw looks into the bag at all the things it holds and he looks up to say something, he knows not what, but the shutter slams closed and he is left there alone.

With his bags Shaw follows the street running alongside the bus station to where it meets highway and from there he follows highway west into night. His walk takes him in and out of the fall of streetlights that give shape to only so much world and in time even these fall away leaving only the man and the highway and the night. Stars form shapes in the sky. Patterns lost in city luminescence now emerge in the unending swath of nothing. He walks for miles. He walks for hours. No cars pass and no change exists in the black and then there is a sound, there is a rumble some miles back that in its own time grows to a roar. Shaw turns to look. Headlights come his way and the churning heart of a steel apparition blooms as it nears until it is there and gone in but a second. And as the weak red taillight recedes to little in the miles ahead, and as that shade exits

and turns down a distant country road, Shaw
looks back at what was seen in the car as it passed.
A light did show and in that faint illumination the
babyfaced man looked out from the passenger
window and into the passing night.

Shaw follows the path of the car off the
highway and down the country road and on. The
buzz of light surrounds. Bugs, trees, wind. The
heat of day is hours gone. A chill settles into bone
and into flesh. Shaw stops along roadside, laying
down his things and fetching and unfolding his
blanket. He places the food bag inside the larger
sack and this he ties to his wrist and he wraps the
blanket around his form like a shawl and he goes
on down the road.

Morning comes as a slow spreading blue, a light
that forms out of nothing. An exhaustion sets in, a
weariness that isn't there and then is, a thing that
comes in waves, dizzying. Shaw's walking slows
but goes on. That thin veil of morning displays the
world, hills in the distance and plains and miles of
road.

A sound familiar and oppressive appears in the
void. Some ways off a car tops a hill and dips
under and tops another. Shaw watches for
minutes at its oncoming rush. It passes as a

snapshot in time. When Shaw closes his eyes he can see that phantom as if it stood still. Muscle car, old, ancient. A sheen of fine dust marks every inch. The driver sat alone in that space.

The sound quiets but does not die away. Shaw stops. He turns. That old muscle car phantom waits. It idles in the middle of the road a quarter mile back. Shaw looks both directions but there is nothing else along the road for miles. There is nothing. A minute passes. There is a flash of taillights as gears change and then that phantom is moving again, shrinking to a point in the miles Shaw has left behind.

He pulls blanket close around his shoulders and turns back to the road but he does not move. He breathes. The sky has lightened and is lightening still. Off the road there is a field of something high and soft, a grass, a grain, something waving in its lackadaisical way as morning breeze wafts. He wades in for a dozen yards and then a dozen more and he stops. He turns back and the road is still there. He sinks down below the grass. He is hungry, he is starving, but that weariness is everything now and he lets it have all of him as wrapped tight in his thick, makeshift shawl he falls into a deep sleep.

3

He watches them for minutes before the last fog of sleep recedes enough for him to understand what it is he sees. Specks move along the surface of the sack holding his things where it lay in the circle of grass flattened by Shaw's hours of reprieve. Those specks resolve into lines and those lines crawl in organized march from sack to greased paper exposed in open bag mouth. Ants.

"No."

Shaw speaks that one word and then he is rising and he's moving and he is taking up that exposed sandwich in its greased paper and flinging it into the distance. He grabs the sack and moves off several paces into the lea and he upends the contents onto the ground. He shakes out the sack and he dusts off and examines each item and one by one they are packed away once more. He returns to where he slept. His blanket is there waiting. He leans down but the floor of earth obscures the ants' provenance.

The clouds do not move. Overhead is a sky of such blue, so still, the backdrop of a stage play. Shaw sits on the blanket and looks up into that forever blue, that utter openness. He closes his eyes and he feels midday sun on his skin and he opens his eyes again. Plastic crackles as he rummages for a sandwich. A passing car is a distant sigh. The boom of a truck hauling freight follows the car. Half the sandwich is gone in two bites. He chews with eyes closed. A noise comes from him, a sound of deep pleasure. When he drinks he drinks a bottle down to its dregs. He tosses away the bottle, he tosses away the paper. He lies back on the blanket and watches the sky but never do those clouds move in that pane of unending blue.

He breathes in deep drafts. He thinks he has fallen asleep again but he has not. He stands and stretches and he gathers the blanket into the larger of the sacks so that as he emerges from the chaff he is trailing a sack from each hand.

He walks. Down that road he walks for a hundred yards but nothing in the landscape has changed, nothing in the sky has changed. He walks for an hour and still the world is unmoved. He wipes his brow with the back of a hand still clutching its purchase and he stops. He sets his things down in pale road dust and he retrieves a water and unscrews the top and drinks. He swallows and breathes and drinks again. He looks at the sun but he cannot guess the time. Midday still.

A distant whisper of tires grows at his back. He turns and waits and a shape coalesces, a box of a car, angles hard and form small, a sedan of a make some years gone. Motor whirs in lawnmower hum. It pulls to a stop in the road alongside Shaw. A man behind the wheel stares across to the passenger window and out as Shaw stares back. The driver leans and he rotates a crank that lowers the window in fits and jerks. When it's down he just stares. He leans a hand on the passenger seat and he looks out at Shaw with furrowed brow.

"You okay out here?"

"I'm okay."

The driver waits for more but Shaw only stands.

"Well. You're out here, miles from, I mean, anything."

Shaw looks each way and he looks at the driver.

"There's road. Where does this road go?"

"Do you need a ride someplace?"

"No."

"Well."

The driver looks into the mirror at the road behind as if to check for traffic he might be blocking but there is nothing for long miles.

"You sure you don't need a ride?"

"I don't."

The driver nods.

"All right, then."

That lawnmower hum carries the box of a car on down the road. Shaw watches it go, but before it has disappeared in those empty miles he has taken up his things and begun his walk again.

***

It's a mirage. It is a thing conjured from dream, from desire. Structures grow on the horizon, the hard angles of old dwellings. When he nears he finds a line of empty storefronts cobbled from wood dried over decades in the sun. Glass remains

in some windows but not all. The logic of how the
unbroken were chosen to be spared is impossible
to know. Beyond the shops is a field upon which a
dozen crumbling shacks are spread. The humble
components of a town. A place between places.
Here and there empty lots tell the story of
something gone, a fence, a change in the grass too
subtle to name. A concrete slab takes up a half
acre. Shaw stands on this, turning in every
direction. He lays down his sacks, he takes off his
coat. A manor house stands back from the rest, a
half mile's walk from the road. Shaw heads off in
its direction.

It is an amalgam. It is a chimera. The manor
house has not the shape of a brownstone or castle
or gothic abode but that of three houses stitched
together, odd, monstrous. A wound shows where
roof meets wall in the manor's north wing, beams
fallen and roofing caved in. Windows caked in
decades of dust display only darkness. He climbs
steps of old wood that groan underfoot and at
their top he finds himself standing at a door as tall
as two men. Black paint has faded to gray where it
has not cracked and peeled away. He puts a hand
on an ivory knob and turns and pushes but there
is no give. He pushes harder but still nothing

happens. He steps back and he steps forward
again. He knocks, he waits. He knocks again.
When he hears nothing inside he descends the
steps.

Pinks and purples have seeped into the sky.
Bruises of cloud. He takes the time to walk around
the house but there is no other door, no other way
in. The caved roofing is far out of reach, the
window glass all intact. When he has finished his
search the last of the sun is bleeding away.

On the walk back to his things Shaw spots a
well set in among the crumbling village. A pump
and a spigot extend from the works and a length of
tin sheeting covers the well proper. A rock holds
the tin in place. He looks this over but in the
onrushing dark there is little to see. He moves on
to retrieve his things.

The house he chooses is decided on by
proximity alone. He sits on a step and he unwraps
a sandwich and in the growing night he takes his
meal. Slow bites, savoring. Sounds he's not heard
since a childhood long put away rise all around, an
orchestra of memory. Insects, wind, a vague
vibration, this nameless presence. The noise of the
world. He eats and he listens.

To the west beyond the road the land climbs
into hills and grassland is overtaken by a line of
trees climbing with those hills so that all that can
be seen in that scenic panorama is the canopy of
green fading into night and in among the
woodland there does shine but a single light.

4

He wakes with throat dry from a night of breathing dust. He swallows hard. He sits up on bare wood. His head hurts. Everything hurts. Floor creaks and joints pop as he stretches and stands. Nothing moves in the room. He sways in the quiet. When he is ready he goes out.

Shaw takes his breakfast on the same step on which he sat eating the night before. He sniffs at the sandwich before he eats and he is unsure what the results of this test suggest. He watches the road as he chews but no cars pass by. A signpost sticks up from the ground but its signage is nowhere, stolen or buried in dust. Down the road another post sticks up and bolted to this pole is a rectangle of green with MILE 43 etched across its front.

He goes house to house exploring. He does it all afternoon. Some rooms are hollowed out, some are left as if their inhabitants have only just stepped away, cabinets full, everything in its place. In some, items are left on floors, shirts or dishes or papers. One building is filled with a chemical stench and glass is spread across the floor.

When he finds a tap he runs it. Some make noise and some do nothing at all but not a one that he tries brings water. He lets them run for minutes, in kitchens, in bathrooms, bathtubs. Nothing. In time he works his way back to the well.

He looks the works over. He leans in close but he has no reference for what it is he is seeing. He lifts the rock and the tin sheeting but the hold below is black. He listens but he hears nothing. He sniffs the air but the air is clear. He puts back tin and rock and returns to the works. He levers the pump a dozen times and water begins to flow from the spigot and he goes on levering the pump for a full minute. He puts a hand under the spigot and leans and sniffs and tastes and the water is clear and sweet. He drinks and turns to breathe and then he drinks again until the water falls to a trickle. When the water stops he wipes his hand on his pants.

There are finds. There are items that call out. Some practical, some not. He drags a mattress to the concrete slab to let the sun wash it clean and in time he turns it over and leaves it again. When he is satisfied he drags it to the house in which he spent the night before. He brings dishware, he brings tools. He brings a carving knife rusted and dull. He finds a photo in humble frame of men standing along a bar, each turned with glass or bottle to look at the camera's flash. This he places on the room's only shelf.

At dusk he sits on the porch. Again he sniffs at the sandwich and again he is unsure what he has learned from the effort. He expects the offended reaction beyond his control, the recoiling elicited by rot, but there is none of this. He opens the bread and peels away the meat all the same. He tosses the meat to the gravel beyond the steps and he eats only the bread.

Off in the hills night finds its way in just as it does here with Shaw. In that night that one light shows while down below Shaw sits only in darkness.

The black into which Shaw wakes is complete. He blinks but there is nothing to see. He does not move. His chest rises and falls with each breath but this movement is detached, the perfunctory machinery of existence whirring in the night.

The sound that matters is outside. The sound outside is everything. It is the world. It is the universe. Snarls and slopping bites and the huffing breaths of animals. Underneath bugs hum. In time the animal sounds fall away and sometime after that comes the howling. Dogs or coyotes. A car passes with the ugly roar of a familiar beast and hours later it passes again and then the night is quiet.

5

He eats chips. He eats snack cakes. When these things are gone he folds and folds again the now-empty plastic sack in which they were held and puts it into a pants pocket. A truck hauling a long trailer goes by on the road and some time later a tractor comes along. A woman of middle age in the cab raises a hand to wave as she goes by in her slow passing. Shaw waves back. He watches as she goes on her way. He drinks water from a bottle refilled at the well and screws the top back on and tosses it through the open door onto his scavenged mattress. Then he rounds the house and heads east.

The manor house sits as it had days before and as it had years before that. Shaw stops at a window and with a sleeve he wipes clean a circle through which to look but all there is to see is a hallway running south to north the length of the house and at the far end a spill of light where the roof has fallen in to display empty space and the aimless swirl of dust.

East again through golden fields. The land slopes downward and scrub and shrubbery create a maze in places. A creek cuts the land. A line of trees follows its course. Waters move along at a trickle. He steps across on the tops of rocks worn smooth, each footfall ginger. On the other side he climbs a bank into more grassland and scrub and in the distance a single tree. As he nears he finds the tree intertwined with a length of chain link fence extending ten feet each way before its ends twist and angle down to lay flat, lost in the field. Trunk grown through links. More bush than tree. Plums hang from flowering shoots. Shaw plucks one of the fruits and he runs a thumb over a waxy film that covers its surface. He takes a bite and another and another. Juice runs and stains sleeve. When he's done he tosses the pit away. He fills a

plastic sack with a dozen or more before he turns
to head back.

When again he comes to the creek he stops. He
looks into the water for things moving there. Fish
and mud creatures. He follows along the land cut
by the creek. A trench of sorts. A hundred yards
on a hole opens in the wall alongside the creek, a
mine like a worm's burrow dug in dirt and clay
and rock. Shaw steps in and stops and listens but
there is nothing but the sound of running water at
his back. He waits. Then he goes back the way he
came.

***

He makes his fire with wood pulled from the ruin
of a collapsed home. He lights straw with his
lighter and he sets it to wood and then he sits
watching. He makes his fire back from the road
and from the houses but any passing car would
still see. He eats a plum in the circle of light
thrown while all around is night.

He hears the footsteps long before they come
near. A patter in the grass, a whisper of cloth. The
man who steps into the light wears work boots,
loose jeans, plain jacket. Unshaven for some

weeks. Hair hanging in greased strips. This wayfarer takes a seat in a spot cleared of grass. He points a finger at the remains of plum in Shaw's hand.

"Where'd you find that?"

Shaw gestures to the darkness at his back.

"There's a tree past the creek."

"Can I have it?"

Shaw looks at the half-eaten plum.

"This?"

"Yes, that."

"I need it."

"You need it."

Shaw nods.

"I hear there's a tree of them out here. Just past the creek."

Shaw eats his plum. When he's done he tosses the pit into the fire. The wayfarer watches that knot black to cinder. He does not talk for some time. When he does speak it is of needs. He says to Shaw some men need a plum and some men need the walk to go get it. He says they need the act, and the act is purpose. A plum is just a plum, it isn't anything. When it is eaten it's gone.

Shaw watches the wayfarer and listens and when the man is done speaking he reaches into a pocket of his plain jacket. What he brings out is a plum. He takes a bite and throws the rest into the fire. He looks at Shaw and he is looking at Shaw and he is waiting. Then he stands and he thanks Shaw for the company and the wayfarer travels on silent feet into the night.

6

He spots them as he is washing his hands. He has gone through his morning necessaries and he's only just come up hair and face running with water drunk straight from the spigot and he is rubbing his hands together in a manner idle and perfunctory when his eyes catch the couple sitting on a blanket spread in the center of the concrete slab. His crouch is instinctual, the posture of an animal. He watches with a wariness. If they have seen him it does not show. She takes a drink from a glass. He spreads something along a hunk of bread and takes a bite. Shaw watches their movements in the distance. When they've turned away he steps between husks of old buildings and is gone.

On his trek through open fields he imagines
weaving grasses together into a crude rope that he
loops and ties in a semblance of a snare, but these
flights lack details vital to the task's execution.
Fantasies of rugged life. A dilettante's
understanding of the pioneer everyday.

At the creek he retrieves a stick from the muck
with a mind to sharpen it into a spear or fasten a
blade to its end to form a rudimentary pike, but he
does none of these things. He leans on the stick
and looks into the water. Surface ripples where
rock breaks through. Now and then comes the dart
of color as a fish goes on its way. Shaw swings the
stick at this movement but the effort only smacks
water. He would make a pole if he had string, if he
had a hook, bait. He swings the stick again but
with no more success than before.

The toad is silent. It sits in the shallows, skin
the color of moss. When Shaw steps near, it
readjusts its position and stills and does not move
again. The stick is swung hard and water splashes
as the stick connects and the toad rolls limp in the
mud. Shaw stands over the green lump waiting
but the toad remains limp, remains unmoving. He
peels one end of the stick, removing strips of the
wood until the end is not sharp but is thin enough

for the task. He pokes the end through the toad's middle and as the wood penetrates flesh there is a slight pop. Shaw sets this aside and climbs the bank and when he returns he carries a handful of grass like straw and a bundle of loose wood pieces. He lays his kindling on a tract of dry ground and he brings out his green lighter and sets fire to the works. He purses his lips and cups the trickle of fire and blows until flame blossoms and spreads. He takes up the stick and holds it just over the flame and he waits. He squats and this goes on. When he pulls back the stick and the toad's flesh has blackened he kicks the little fire into the creek, sticks and flame and all. With thumb and pointer he pulls toad from stick's end.

The bite is a crunch and then it is bitter mush and Shaw gags and swallows and spits. This is not meat. This is not meat. He drops what remains of the toad and for a full minute he stands sweating and breathing. When he vomits it is violent and without control. He falls to his knees in the mud and his body erupts. After the convulsions stop and he can again breathe he stands and he climbs the bank and enters the grassland.

His heart is racing. His vision shimmers. The world before him is a desert mirage. It is a silver glare of starshine in day and then little by little the world retreats as color fades and detail gives way to soft blues. The manor house is there and beyond that the village and then it is not as the world has gone black. Still his body moves. He is saying words or he thinks he is. He stumbles and he falls to one knee and he stands again, he moves again. The next time he stumbles he cannot stand. The world becomes fire. He does not recall the change, the shift from a black nothing to the deluge of oranges and reds. He is speaking again. His voice is swallowed by the jungle roar of a beast he cannot see but whose call envelops the world.

***

When he wakes he gasps and swallows and closes his eyes again. Somewhere there is a voice speaking but this is a noise distant and indistinct. He breathes. Another voice joins the first. A man and a woman. Disjointed talk.

"It's an hour away, easy."

And.

"We don't even know him."

And.

"He's breathing fine. He's okay now."

49

Snippets. Shaw makes a noise like a word. When their talk at once quiets he opens his eyes. A boy and a girl of maybe twenty something. She looks at Shaw and then she looks at the boy. She is saying go, she is saying he needs it. The boy disappears and the girl kneels and she says something Shaw does not understand. In time he sits up and she asks his name and he tells her and he does not ask hers. She asks if he needs anything and he says he just got sick, he just got sick. The boy returns with a bowl scrounged from some ruin and water held within and Shaw sits drinking for some time in silence. When he talks he says thank you and he waits. The girl says he needs to go to a hospital and he says no. He again says thank you.

"Come on."

The boy. The look the girl turns on the boy at his words is annoyance or more than annoyance. The boy stands silent now, chastened. Shaw does not look at them, at either of them. He looks at his little town spread out on the plain and he says you can go, he says it's okay if you go.

7

There are more stars here. Thousands more. Millions. A painting once perfect which in other locales has faded under a light harsh and constant.

Shaw sits eating a plum under the stars. He sits on the step of his home. An owl calls out and something shuffles in the trees and those million stars do shine. When a car passes on the road he does not move and the light passes over him as it does all things and he is unseen there, another piece of night.

The light is there in the hills. Shaw stares unblinking and waits and in time he cannot know if it moves or sits changeless. When his plum is gone Shaw tosses away the pit and wipes his hands on his pants and then he has another.

The next night is the same. The light, the plums. It is there always, a window into a world of fire existing just on the other side of reality. A pinhole in the fabric of night. He watches and he waits for some tangible shift, some clarity. In time he goes inside and sleeps.

In the morning he rises and readies himself and then he stands alongside the road. He looks across at the hills and at the place in the hills where in the night that light burned. It's all different now. The world has shapes absent in the black. In day it takes on forms distinct and textured where before there was nothing but the black and the light and the crystalline shimmer above. He closes his eyes and orients himself in that facsimile of night and when he is satisfied he opens them and sets off.

The air is different under the trees. Thick and sweet and fertile. Each footfall comes with the crisp snap of things crushed. Leaves, brush. And loud, as if there is at once less sound and more of every sound there is. His breath comes heavy. In time it is strained. In time he is huffing. He leans as he walks but if he is climbing or descending he does not know. He looks to the canopy above but everything is the same. He stops and with eyes closed he listens. The world slows. His breath deepens. When he is walking again he is climbing, he is moving in what he thinks is a northwest slant.

The trees open onto a half acre of cleared land. Sun falls on meandering vines and leafy greens and here and there a tree of a different sort. Pecan, apple. Shaw steps forward to feel that sun on his skin but he does not linger in this place. The sound of a car comes from the road. Smooth whoosh of engine and brakes and gravel. Shaw heads that way, stumbling down.

He stops at the tree line. He watches. Parked at the roadside sits an amalgam, a pastiche. Curved lights and long-bodied, angular and teal. Like a mix of a past and a future. Like a memory of a roadster. Like a rocket in an old movie. The trunk gapes open and alongside the roadster stands the girl. She leans down and in and after a moment she straightens again. In her hand a plastic sack. She enters the open field where ahead of her walks the boy. He carries a box or a package. When he gets to the manor house he climbs the steps and places his bundle on the porch. The girl does the same with hers. He returns to the car and she returns to the car and they each take up more items to unload.

Shaw waits. He watches for minutes. When they are back in the roadster with she in the driver's seat and he in the passenger's they sit talking. There is nodding, there is pointing. They are discussing waiting. They are discussing Shaw. Then the boy is looking down. He looks down for some time. When he looks up again he says something to the girl and then he is opening his door, he is stepping out and jogging his way to the manor house once more. He pauses, then he steps to the wall and seems to adjust something there. When this is done he jogs back to the roadster and slams shut the door and they are pulling onto the road, they are driving away.

Shaw waits to move until the roadster is vanished in its entirety and then he steps from the trees and crosses the road and with unhurried pace he makes the walk to the manor house. At the top of those ancient steps sit cases of canned goods wrapped thick with plastic film. Soups, vegetables. A box of spring water with the rest. Among it all there sits a plastic sack. Shaw looks inside and finds instruments of daily life. Matches, candles, toothbrush, can opener. Underneath it all a paperback, a tattered mystery. Shaw drags the cans behind the porch railing and he drags the water there too and the plastic sack he takes up and holds.

On the wall a note hangs from a nail. With the note a pen, suspended by its cap. Shaw steps near and reads careful script. Do you need anything? Shaw takes the pen and removes the cap and beneath the boy's words he writes no.

***

He reads by candlelight. The old mattress is worn and stiff but there is comfort there. Each subtle shift brings an earned groan of springs. The shadows sway but it's enough light. Just enough. Shaw licks a finger and turns a page.

He hears it in plenty of time. That distant roar, that bestial tumult. He hears it coming but he does not move. He cannot. That rumble approaches and it grows and then it is there, not passing, stopped. It waits alongside the town.

His paralysis breaks. When Shaw moves he moves fast. He drops the paperback and rolls from bed and in stooped rush he moves to the candle. Hand cups flame and he blows. Now there is darkness. Now nothing moves. Still that phantom waits. That chugging idle. Shaw wants to look, to move to a window and peek with one eye, but he does not. He waits, crouched against a wall. When the thud of gears shifting comes and that engine roars away still he does not move. For some time the only sound is Shaw's measured breathing, but little by little the established noises of night do return.

8

The next time he goes it is night. The light is there to follow. It is there in the hills like a beacon and it is there as he crosses the street but as he wades into waves of wooded climb that signal becomes obscured. Shaw moves ever onward toward that light or toward the idea of it, the place where something in him believes it to be. There is an instinct present in the night, something in him pointing the way, a thing which in the day had no voice.

The woodland breathes in those hills, a measured inhale and exhale of the world. Night sounds are a chorus here. They are a symphony. Shaw is a part of that symphony. The brush of shoe, the snap of wood. The ringing in his ears. The fears he holds tight to. Then the song changes. Ground hardens underfoot and air opens around him and a corridor of black has appeared running up and running down. He turns again to the climb. Now a path defines his steps. The trail winds and Shaw follows its subtle shifts by feel and some arcane knack until ahead the way opens onto a place of thinned growth. Trees dot the land still but here the canopy is diminished and moon above touches the face of a house at the far end of the clearing. A single window is lit with soft glow. Other structures loom in the wood. No light shows in these from window or moon. Growth sprouts all around these darkened forms. Some structures seem to slump or lean and some seem to have altogether fallen.

Shaw stops at the border of this place. He waits for some change that does not come. That window is there. That steady light. There is no waver or candle flicker, only a square of plank wall illuminated in that frame. Minutes pass. In time Shaw turns away.

He follows the trail back down. When it breaks upon road it does so north of town. Shaw walks along the roadside back to his home where he goes in and lays on the old mattress there and with his coat pulled around him in seconds he sleeps.

He lays a sack of gathered plums on the creek's
bank and lowers himself onto a rock set in place
and sucked down into mud for long years. He
takes the carving knife from a scabbard made from
a piece of old curtain and lashed to his belt with a
strip of the same. He takes up a limb broken off
from the plum tree and with the knife's blade he
shaves and sharpens the stick. When the point is
needle fine he returns the knife to its sheath and
he removes shoes and socks and rolls up pants
above ankles and with the stick he wades into the
creek. Time passes. He stands so still. When a
ripple shows or when color flashes or when a
bubble breaks the surface he stabs with his spear.
Over and over he tries. All afternoon he tries. His
labors produce only frustration. In time he
abandons the spear with a toss and he goes to
slashing at movement in the water with the
carving knife but this endeavor is as fruitless as
the one that went before.

The sun is falling away from the world when he
crosses back across the open field with his bag of
plums and nothing more. When he reaches the
manor house he stops and turns and he climbs the
warped steps to the porch. The note hangs from
its nail. Shaw takes up the pen and marks a line

through his no and then he marks another so that
the no is crossed out and beneath this he adds a
new note. Fishing pole.

***

He follows the trail up from the road. A shining
moon lights the sky. Clouds radiate with that light
and underneath Shaw walks in this pale
illumination. In each hand a plum. As he nears
the clearing he steps off the trail and moves
between the trees until he sees the window and
the light held there. He sits down there beneath
the trees. After a time he eats a plum and tosses
away the pit and he waits. The moon moves in its
slow way.

A shadow moves along the wall in that window
and Shaw tenses. He sits forward but no one
appears. He closes his eyes and maybe he sleeps
and maybe he does not. When he opens his eyes a
song is playing. Something old, swing or jazz, all
brass and life. He cannot hear its delicate contours
through distance and night and wood cabin wall
but he hears enough to know it for something he
has heard before, some forgotten standard. His
eyes close again and in time the music ends.

9

He has no soap. He runs his clothes under the well's spigot and he scrubs each article first with knuckles and then with those pieces already wettened. When he is satisfied with each piece he moves nude with it to the concrete slab and lays it flat in the sun to dry, pants and shirt and socks and shorts. Stones hold clothes in place. His shoes are left there with the rest. If someone comes along as he crosses the field he will pretend he does not notice their passing by but no one comes along. He returns to the well to wash himself as best he can.

Days of grit stain skin creases. He wrings filth from limbs and he kneels and lets the fall of water wash over him, soaking hair and flesh, ears filling one and then the other. He does not hear the phantom engine rumble but he feels the ground

quiver. Eyes that were closed now open. He
shakes his head in a motion of fury. He listens but
he hears only the fall of water. A hand darts out to
shut off the spigot. A trickle still runs but that
rumble is there. He tries to breathe but he cannot.
He tries to think but the dread that grips does not
wait and he is running, he is in the field and
running, screened by the dot of each humble
structure at his back. Grasses whip skin. He is out
of breath but still he runs. There is a clarity of
thought in which he asks himself why he runs and
he cannot answer this. Still he runs. His body runs
and his very being exists in a fog of blind panic
but within him he sits with these questions trying
only to understand.

And the creek is there. He stumbles through
brush and down the bank and he follows the
snaking flow to the hole cut in rock wall and here
he steps into the dark. He stops. His pulse
thunders. He takes another step, and another, and
another. All is shadow here. He turns and leans
against rock and he sinks to the ground. In time
he can breathe again. In time his pulse calms.

The rock is slick with damp. He cannot see the
mud on his feet but he feels it when he curls toes
and when it dries and flakes he feels it again. The

sound is all wrong here. The gurgle of water's travel echoes and somewhere in the dark of that tunnel dug deep into the earth there is a breath that goes on unending.

He pulls his feet under him and he waits. He looks at himself but there is so little to see. The idea of a form. The dark is thick here. It seems to spread like ink spilled. He untucks his legs and lays them out before him. The paleness of those limbs is almost lost. Above them a wall. He stares but what is there is only black. He thinks of this place. He thinks of the people who might have come before. Did they leave their stories on the walls? Are those stories there now if only there was light to see? He stares. The darkness seems to move but no picture resolves.

Shaw closes his eyes. The change is negligible. He thinks of the things that live here now. Things that crawl, things that slither. He imagines the tickle of limbs like hairs brushing his skin. He dozes and he waits.

Night has come when he steps into the creek. He splashes himself and wrings his skin again and he wipes his face with wet hands. He climbs the bank and he crosses the field and under the shine of silver moon he returns to town. His clothes are where he left them. He moves the stones aside and gathers his things and carries them with him to the little house he's taken for his own. Nothing is moved, nothing is touched. As if that phantom throwback of a car with its roaring taunt was never there.

***

It is still night when he rises. What must be hours have gone by as he has sat in bed wrapped in his coat and waiting for a sleep that has not come. He dresses in the dark and he steps out and moves up the road and follows the trail into the hills to the cabin. There is no music, but the light in the window is there. He sits among the trees. He has no plums with him now. He has brought nothing with him. He sits watching that light in the dark. His eyes fall shut all on their own.

He wakes in blue morning. The sun makes its way through the canopy in pale sheets, diaphanous, spilling down as if poured. Birdsong comes from all around.

The man standing over Shaw shows a frown. The lines of middle-age shape his features. His suit is well made but simple, well kept but aged,

64

fading. He wears his hair in the archaic undercut of a jazz player or revolutionary. The man asks Shaw if he is from the board and Shaw does not respond. The man kneels. He puts hands on knees and balances and he looks at Shaw. He says nothing and Shaw says nothing and the man stands again.

"Well, come on, then."

The man turns and he moves off toward the cabin. Shaw stands. He dusts himself off and wipes hands on pants and he follows.

The cabin door swings wide and the man steps into the warm glow of a bare bulb screwed into a vase the color of coal. He motions at the door and he says to leave it open and Shaw does. Shaw enters a room cluttered with too much furniture for rooms so modest; an overlarge recliner, filing cabinets, tables, more. A record player sits on a desk.

"Sit."

Shaw moves to the recliner. A blanket knitted in cold colors lays draped across the arms. This Shaw takes up and folds over the chairback. He sits. The man is pouring water from a jug into a black tower with a spigot that in seconds dribbles out enough coffee to fill one mug.

"Coffee?"

Shaw says no, he says thank you. The man pours from the jug again and fills with coffee a second mug identical to the first and he hands this to Shaw.

"It's ungracious to say no to hospitality. Somebody offers you a cup of coffee, you take it. You don't have to drink it, but you take it."

"It's ungracious to point out ungraciousness."

The man pulls out a desk chair and he sits.

"It is that."

Time passes in quiet. Shaw holds the hot mug in two hands. He looks at the swirl of oil brew, steam rising. When he speaks he says he can't drink it.

"You can't drink it. Why can't you drink it?"

Shaw tells the man he's eaten only plums for days. The man repeats the word. Plums. Shaw nods and the man asks him if he has any other food and he says no, he says he does not. Then he shakes his head and he tells the man he has some cans but they don't belong to him.

"I think whoever they belong to would understand."

Shaw sits looking at the man. A beat goes by and then the man is standing and he is setting

down his mug and stepping through a narrow
doorway into a little room holding cabinets and an
icebox and utensils hanging from pegs. He takes
down a pan and a long spatula with a wooden
handle and he steps behind a wall where there
comes a clamor of activity. The woof of flame
igniting. Something begins to sizzle. Shaw looks at
the mug in his hands. He speaks without looking
up. He asks the man if this is his home and from
the little kitchen the man says this is all his. This
is his town. These are his hills, his mines, his
fields. He calls himself an heir. He says he
inherited this world.

When the heir returns from the little kitchen
he carries with him a plate of eggs scrambled and
mixed with greens. Shaw sets the coffee
untouched on the desk and he sets the plate
across his knees. He takes up a fork from the
plate. The grip is carved with intricate designs.
The forms of angels. The fork is heavy in his hand.
Shaw holds it out before him.

"Where did the eggs come from?"

"Where?"

"I didn't see a chicken."

The heir says there is a chicken. He says there's
a garden too. Shaw begins to eat and for some

time the only sounds are the artless scrape of cutlery and wet chewing. The heir sits in the desk chair and takes up his coffee and drinks it and when it is gone he drinks Shaw's too.

Shaw eats until the plate is clean. He sets the fork on the empty plate. The coffeemaker lets out a hiss but no drop falls. Shaw asks the heir if he can have another cup.

10

Shaw climbs the trail before the sun has come up. That light glows there in the window. At the door he waits, he listens. Movement sounds somewhere on the other side, a shuffling, a scraping. He knocks. When the door opens the heir nods and waves Shaw to the recliner and he moves off to the little kitchen. Now comes the sound of stirring, spoon on pan. Shaw sits and he waits. The heir calls from the kitchen, he asks Shaw what it is he wants.

"I don't know. I don't want anything."

"Everybody wants something."

"I haven't seen many people out here."

The heir makes a noise, a grunt.

"There it is. You're looking for conversation. Human interaction."

Shaw shakes his head.

"I'm not."

The heir comes into the front room with a black ceramic bowl in each hand. He pulls out the desk chair with a foot and hands Shaw a bowl and he sits. A spoon protrudes from thick oatmeal. Shaw stirs and scoops and tastes. Sugar, cinnamon, butter. The heir is looking at him.

"Do you live out here?"

Shaw nods, he says he does.

"I have a house down by the road."

The heir watches him with eyes hard.

"But the house is mine. The road is mine."

Shaw looks at the heir and for a moment there is quiet. The heir goes on with his staring. A vague tremor shakes the hand holding spoon. Then he is repeating his questions, he is asking Shaw what he wants.

"Another life. If I'm making wishes I want another life."

The heir considers this. Then he nods and he stands and asks Shaw to excuse him a moment. He opens a door and closes it behind him and here Shaw sits alone in the front room. He sets down his bowl next to where the heir left his own on the desk.

Talk comes from behind the door. Shaw moves close and listens but the sound is all rounded and shaved. He cups his ear to the door but gets nothing. He moves back to the desk. Hands and eyes wander over items there. He moves aside a pen and takes up a notebook and flips through pages of scribbled text. Not a manifesto but more than a journal. Events real or imagined march one after another with assumed results adding to the measure of the next round of plot.

The door opens.

"That's not for you."

The heir takes the notebook from Shaw's hands and returns it closed to the desk and with care he sets the pen back on its cover.

"You writing a book?"

"What?"

"That looks like the outline for a book."

The heir stares a moment. He says no. He says it's a plan to make a point. He says he is going to show some men in some tower who owns this place that it can make money again. For them it's a write-off, its worth more if it stays dead. But it doesn't have to.

Shaw listens to these things and he takes it all in and when the heir's speech has ended he speaks up.

"But this place is yours."

The heir is quiet.

"How can men in a tower have any say if this is all yours?"

For a moment the heir's hard eyes change and his jaw is set and his fingers are curling into a fist. Then he takes a breath and another and he says thank you for the visit. Shaw doesn't move. He looks at the man, looking for something there. At last he speaks.

"Do you have any books?"

"So it's books you want now."

Shaw shrugs.

"What'll you trade me?"

"I don't have anything."

"Trade me a favor."

"I'll trade you a book for a book. One for one."

The heir shakes his head no but what he says to Shaw is I'll think about it.

11

Shaw climbs the trail in the morning with a book in his hand. The paperback mystery. When he knocks at the cabin door the heir shouts back.

"Is that you?"

And.

"Come on in."

When he presses through the door Shaw steps into a fog of scents, spices and meats and something. Carrots, something. Onions. The heir is in the kitchenette with his scraping and stirring. He speaks words that Shaw doesn't hear. Shaw holds up the paperback.

"I brought a book."

"What?"

The heir leans into the room. Shaw holds up the paperback again.

"A book."

The heir waves an overly large spoon at nothing in particular and turns back to his work. After a moment there comes the clang of that utensil or another and then the sound of pouring and the heir steps into the room with the same black bowls. What is held in the bowl he hands to Shaw is some kind of stew, chunks of color swirling in greased broth. Steam rises. Shaw tries to taste but the broth burns. He blows across the stew's surface while the heir slurps his down. Between bites the heir speaks.

"You see a dog? A girl came to my door looking for a dog."

"A girl?"

"A kid. A child."

"Where did she come from?"

The heir points around with his spoon.

"The hills, I'd guess."

"I haven't seen anybody."

The heir shakes his head.

"They're out there."

Shaw blows on his stew. He spoons broth into his mouth and swallows and blows on the surface again. For a moment he eats in the quiet but the heir is already done with his meal.

"Let's see that book."

Shaw passes over the paperback and the heir turns it in his hands. He turns pages to legal information and he reads and he turns it over again. He nods.

"Okay."

He stands and leaves the room and when he returns the book he carries is another altogether. Shaw takes it and looks it over and there on the cover is a tree ancient and twisted and massive and from which a limb hangs a length of rope tied in a noose.

"It's a western."

Shaw taps the book on his knee and says thank you and he takes a bite of stew. After he swallows he speaks up again.

"Do you have any toilet paper?"

"Toilet paper. Are you shitting me?"

"Is that a joke?"

The heir's face is stone.

"I have some. What'll you trade me?"

"I don't have anything," says Shaw. He holds up the paperback. "I have a book."

The heir doesn't laugh but his face twitches and maybe there is a laugh there.

"I can get you plums."

"Plums from where?"

"I know a place."

"You know a place that is mine. Anyway, I don't need plums. There's a garden south of here. It's where the stuff in that bowl came from."

"Whose garden?"

"My garden."

"But who tends it?"

"Some hill person."

"I don't know what that means."

"The people in the hills have always been there."

Shaw nods and he finishes his stew. He hands the heir the empty bowl. The heir stands as if waiting for something.

"Toilet paper," says Shaw.

The heir sets the bowl on the desktop and again leaves the room and seconds pass and then he is back with a single roll that he hands to Shaw. The heir shows a grin.

"If you're not careful these favors you owe me will add up."

Shaw comes down the trail. He lies on his scrounged mattress with his coat rolled and folded behind his head and he lets his eyes run across the paperback's words. He licks a finger and turns a page. He licks a finger and turns a page. The heir called it a western but the story Shaw finds in that borrowed book is one of horror and dismay.

An engine offers its murmur as it idles nearby. A car door shuts and another slams and voices discuss a thought too soft to hear. The girl, the boy. Shaw closes his eyes and rests the book on his chest but he cannot make sense of their words. In time they recede and some minutes later they return. The car doors shut with some gentleness now. The roadster's hum brightens and moves off in the world and Shaw lifts his book to read again.

12

Shaw climbs the trail and the heir feeds him linguine and butter sauce. He climbs the trail and he eats olives from a jar. Elaborate sandwiches, fish paste on saltines.

Shaw climbs the trail and he trades a paperback for another, and he trades that one for another still. He climbs the trail and he listens to the heir talk of the mines and the history of the mines. He listens to the heir talk of faces and names long gone and significances they had in events all forgotten. The heir talks in language mannered and often polite but in words and phrases that careful presentation of decorum does slip and a stark rage underneath shows through. He talks of lives, of histories. At times the stories contradict those which have come before. Sometimes he is an heir and sometimes he is the last of something. Sometimes the land is his and sometimes it has been stolen away. Sometimes these stories run together until it becomes impossible to discern just which one is that moment's truth.

Shaw climbs the trail to the cabin before the sun is up and the heir is there awake. The heir is always awake.

***

He stops when he sees it, the car parked along the road to the north. Unfamiliar. A long boat of a car. It waits where trail ends in road. Shaw goes that way.

A door is dented and rust eats old steel in patches. He leans to look through the window's dust. Papers and maps and trash lay scattered on the seat and floor. Cups, bags, napkins. He straightens, he looks around. The road lies empty in each direction. Somewhere a bird calls and another answers. Shaw climbs the trail.

Just before the clearing he halts. The cabin door stands open and voices drift out but what they carry is only the sense of talk, an inarticulate rise and fall of murmur that now and then reveals a word. Shaw steps into the trees and then he steps farther still and he waits. When the talk falls away and a stranger emerges from the cabin that stranger is flashes of color seen through the trees and the clop of heavy tread in the clearing and on the trail and down. Shaw stands so still. When in time a car engine starts down below and pulls away and recedes at last Shaw moves.

The cabin door is still open. He moves near in no hurry, listening. In the doorway he stops and squints into the dimmed front room. There at the desk sits the heir. He looks up at Shaw and he looks down again. Rigid back, hands on knees.

"It's not a good time."

Shaw stands at the door looking in.

"It's not a good time."

He lingers there, some thought unformed readying to be spoken when the heir speaks again.

"Come back tomorrow. I may have something for you."

And after a moment.

"A chance."

Shaw nods but the heir isn't looking. Shaw turns and he moves off down the trail. At the road he stops, and though he has all the time he needs he does wait for the tractor heading north and the woman in its cab to make their slow way by. As before she gives a wave and as before Shaw waves back and for some time Shaw watches that tractor shrink in the distance as the guttural chugging of its engine dies away. When it is gone he crosses the road and enters the little house there and he wedges the door shut with a rock.

***

Shaw climbs the trail in the dark. Lamplight falls out through the open door. He passes the threshold into an empty room. A notebook sits open on the cluttered desk. The air carries the pleasing scent of fire.

"Are you here?"

A closed door opens and the heir comes grinning into the room. He holds a glass in loose grip and he slumps into the recliner without speaking to Shaw or looking at Shaw. He gestures with the class to a point somewhere ahead of him and says for Shaw to sit. Shaw does not sit. The heir says he has an idea and he calls it a plan and he asks Shaw if he can drive a truck.

"A truck."

The heir nods and says yeah, yes, and he tells Shaw to get a drink. Shaw does not move. The heir talks of the mines. He talks of reopening the minds. He talks of red tape and of cutting that red tape or charming it or buying it off. He talks of a future, a life. He says for Shaw to have a drink. A moment passes in quiet. Then the heir is lurching to his feet and he is crossing the room as a creature possessed, the demon compelling onward those bones unpracticed in natural motion. In the kitchenette he pauses. He drinks down his drink and pours full the glass from a bottle on the counter and he does not get one for Shaw.

Back in the front room the heir remains standing. Now he talks with his hands. He talks of family. He talks of centuries of sins, and some of them are righteous, and some of them are not. He cites arcane law and he makes reference to Justinian I and he takes hard gulps from the liquid in his glass.

Shaw nods along. He watches the march of this sweeping opera as it plays out around the room. But when again the heir asks him if he can drive a truck Shaw says to the man no, he says he cannot. The heir begins to shout. He shouts curses, curses upon Shaw and upon those he has known or will ever know. He goes on shouting but Shaw has turned and he walks out of the cabin and across the clearing and as he enters the trail down he hears at his back the clap of a door slamming shut.

13

Shaw climbs the trail. When he enters the cabin he finds quiet there. He calls out but he is alone in this place. He waits. He stands so still. The open door lets in the sound of the world. As he leaves he shuts the door behind him.

When he comes again it is another day but the little room is unchanged. Dim light warms the cabin but there is a stillness, the held breath of a place left empty. Shaw falls into the oversized recliner and air and dust do dance. He looks at the front door now closed. He shuts his eyes. He sleeps and he wakes. Outside the room's window the sun has gone and the glow of the bare bulb is the only light in this place. Shaw stands and walks through the narrow doorway and under an arch and in all the days he has come to this place he has never been in the kitchenette before. He turns. He surveys. A dish drainer holds twos. Two plates, two mugs, forks, spoons, knives. A box on the floor is labeled with the word KITCHENWARE. Inside cabinets wait lines of non-perishables. Canned soups, cereals, scotch. He rummages for coffee and when it is found he retreats to the living room with its desk and its coffeemaker. He packs the machine with the tube of crystals and he goes to hit a button but stops, pauses. He moves again to the kitchenette for a mug and for water which he pours into the waiting device before once more going at the button. The maker hums and spurts and in seconds the mug is full. He sits again in the recliner.

The room has changed. In some fashion more felt than seen there is a tone now, something alive that hours before was not. Shaw sips. He looks at the front door. He stands.

The record player on the desk has a switch on its side. Shaw flips it on and flips it off. A stack of records sit amid a jumble of files and books and old paperwork. He flips through their ranks and at random he pulls. He takes the record from its sleeve and he lays it on the player. He moves the needle, he flips the switch. The song that screams

forth is the pain of some crooner in some lounge
long ago. The noise permeates. Shaw closes his
eyes and listens. He opens them.

The kitchenette again. That cabinet, that
scotch. The label says aged. It says 25 years. He
fills his mug and drinks it down and he fills it
again. He takes the bottle with him to the recliner.

The song is replaced by another and then
another still. Shaw listens and he drinks and he
waits. He waits first for the heir to return and then
for some other shift, some event he cannot name
but with every moment he does expect. He lets his
eyes fall closed again and he waits still. Each
breath deepens. A song ends and no other takes
its place and soon the only thing alive in this place
is the player and its white noise as the needle
explores a record's contours.

***

He groans. He touches a hand to his face and he
rises. The song of birds is impossibly loud.
Outside the cabin the sun shines white. In
through the window it falls in long, pale square.
The record spins in place. He toggles the switch
and it stops.

85

He goes through cabinets until he again finds cereal. Shredded wheat. The fridge huffs as he pulls open the door. A machine noise whirs inside. The milk he takes from a shelf is held in a glass bottle with no label. He sniffs at the bottle and he nods. He shoves cereal into his mouth a square at a time and he chases each bite with a swig of milk. He eats standing in the kitchenette with eyes closed. When he has had his fill he leaves box and bottle on the counter by a pristine sink.

He walks in circles in the little front room. He looks at his feet or he looks at nothing. Sometimes he stops to look at a door, the front door or the room's other door closed to he knows not what. He stops to look at things on his trek, items buried in the rubble of years. Papers, photos. He picks them up and puts them down but he is not seeing these things. In time he stops at a door and that door is the front door and he turns the knob and he steps out and breathes. The air is sweet. It is cool but not cold. Breeze caresses the land. Trees stir and skin tightens. A car passes on the road below. Shaw steps back from the doorway and pushes closed the door.

The bottle waits on the floor by the recliner. There was a cork but this is gone. He takes it up and takes a sip and he sets the bottle on the desk. The record goes into a sleeve and another is laid on the player and when a song plays it is something up-tempo, some big band number with no singer, just orchestra and fire. He takes the bottle to the room's other door.

Before he goes in he listens. There is no sound but the song as it plays and still he tries. Seconds pass and when nothing changes he opens the door.

A light is on, a bare bulb much like the other in a lamp made of wood, long and thin, what might have once been a coat rack. A bed takes up most of the room. Sheets are spread flat, loose but near made. Shelves line two walls floor to ceiling. Each row is stacked deep. Books, magazines, folders, binders. Shaw pulls items and flips through their pages. Accounting for businesses long defunct lie mixed among deeds to hovels or invoices for equipment and machinery now rusted or scrapped. Over and over the name Sinclair. Photos of dead men fill albums, pictures of their histories in tones of gray. Those faces smile and drink. There is no order here. The arrangement of things is guided by no one. As if put in place at random. As if set aside to be forgotten. The things Shaw picks up he puts back in their place, as if preserving the timeline that chaos creates.

A closet door stands open. Shaw circles the bed and steps into the open doorway. His body bars the throw of light, and if there is a switch or pull in the darkened cove he does not find it. He waits, he stares. He sips from the bottle. The room coalesces in time. Suits hang on a line with their trousers folded and laid along a shelf and a thick fall of dust lays accumulated on every surface. Farther along the dark is still too thick and what it hides remains hidden. Shaw retreats to the bedroom.

There is no television. There is no phone. A small square of dresser fills a corner. Shaw opens its drawers to find more piled detritus. He lifts back layers and there among pens and coins is a cigarette pack, is a lighter. He takes these things only and returns the drawer to its place.

A shelf on a bedback holds notebooks. This and nothing else. Shaw takes one and in its place he leaves the bottle. He shakes a cigarette from the pack and he lights it and pack and lighter go down on the shelf too. He turns a notebook page. He walks as he reads. Smoke trails in the wake of his passage. He turns a page. At times it is a diary, at times it is plotting. Schemes half-conceived meander along for pages, only to end with no culmination. An abrupt ceasing followed by the next effort and the next. He walks. He walks in and out of rooms. When the cigarette is burned away he lights another. He drinks. He walks. The square of light on the front room's floor moves and is gone and in time is there again. He puts away a notebook and picks up another. He steps into a tiny bathroom with commode and sink and no shower, no bath. He drinks from the tap. He looks at himself in the mirror. A face swathed in beard looks back. Eyes sunken and tired. He steps out again.

He sleeps in the chair when he sleeps. The recliner. He drinks and he smokes and when he remembers to he eats. Milk curdles and he moves to cold cuts in a refrigerator drawer and then cans and then oats. Mostly he reads. The notebooks and files and photos tell the story of a people and a town and the mines fed by both. He follows the rise and fall of a township and a firm and a house. In their brittle pages is a history these things together make. He dreams of them. Those people, those lives. In the recliner he sleeps and he sees those long-ago strangers, and sometimes he is among them, and sometimes he is apart, only watching, a stranger himself or something else, a ghost, a phantom with its ominous circling at the border of their existence.

He wakes. That spill of sun on the floor is there. That shine. It radiates an intensity different from before. Shaw looks at the floor and the sun and he looks at the window. The trees sway and the rest of the world is altogether still, but something has changed. Shaw breathes. He does not get it and then he does. The hum of the fridge is gone. The glow of the lamp. The power is gone and the cabin is still, a relic now, like everything else in this place.

14

He drags down books and bedding and scotch. All he can of each. And toilet paper, roll after roll. He brings these things to his little house in the crumbling town by the road and he arranges them around his meager belongings left untouched in weeks. He has no shelves for books. He stacks paperbacks and more against a wall in tall piles of no contrived order. He straightens these towers and presses and packs them so they themselves make a wall.

He turns in a circle. He takes in his little house. An accumulation of detritus lays where he left it somewhere along the way. Water bottles, wax paper, the leavings of the everyday. He rounds the room and takes each piece of refuse in hand, shoving it into a plastic sack with the name of a chain store written on its side in bold text. When

he is done he ties closed the sack. One last turn
and look and then he is moving and then he is out
the door. He moves between decrepit husks of
homes to a structure long ago caved in and here
atop the piled beams and splintered frame he
tosses his sack of waste.

The manor house. It waits in the distance,
isolated from the remains of the town. A
monument to things gone. Shaw stands looking
off to the east at that stalwart visage ignorant of
the slow faltering of all things. The house is still
and all is still but a hawk with wings spread wide
wandering along the edge of the sky. A minute
passes and another after that. When Shaw moves
he moves into the open field and on to the place
where the first step ends grassland. He puts a foot
on that step and the next and the next. A plastic
case waits at the top of the steps. A box thin and
long sits alongside, cardboard warped by weeks in
the sun, maybe a rain. The exterior of the case is
opaque and the shapes inside are without
meaning. The box is plain, featureless save for
strips of tape holding it together, and this only
just.

Shaw kneels. He unlatches a clasp on the case
and lifts the lid. He rummages through the

contents of a tray and of another beneath the first.
Items are divided among slots of varied sizes.
Plastic fish and rubber worms. Hooks and aspirin
and bandages with adhesive. Each lure is molded
in colors bright and flecked with a vibrant silver.
Shaw removes a pamphlet tucked between trays.
He returns trays and lures to the case and he shuts
and clasps the lid.

The box. He reaches out and at the barest
provocation the strained adhesive gives and two
lengths of polymer come rolling out onto the
porch. The makings of a rod and reel. He turns
and shifts what is left of the box and among the
remains sits a book, sits a bulb of plastic holding
its wound yards of line. He takes the book and
returns the polymer sections of rod to the
unbound box and he drags box and case behind
the porch railing where bottled water and canned
foods still remain. He holds up pamphlet and
book but he does not look at these things and after
a moment that arm falls to his side. He looks
around at the porch. As he moves toward the steps
he pauses. He turns to the door. The note is
changed. The old sheet is gone and in its place is
another with on its face the digits of a phone
number written without breaks or dashes or

parentheses. He leaves the note there on its peg. It stirs in a wind but stays bolted in place.

Back across the field. As he walks he again holds up pamphlet and book but he sees these things no more now than he did before. In the house by the road he falls onto the mattress sheathed in procured bedding and he makes his idle way through the book he's brought with him. No method drives his perusing. He turns pages and lets his eyes wander and he turns more. Anecdotes about crops and tilling are mixed in among step-by-step methods for casting a line or collecting bait. A hodgepodge of essays on fishing and farming. Shaw closes his eyes while holding the book. After a moment he slips the pamphlet in among the pages. He shuts the books and rolls off the bed.

He still holds the book as he climbs the trail. He holds it as he enters the darkened cabin and as he crosses the cluttered front room. He tosses the book onto the seat of the recliner and lays hands on each end of the chairback. He leans and rocks the chair in place where it creaks as its supports break from ruts made over long years. With grunts and groans he drags the recliner from the cabin and he drags it down the trail and as he pulls it

along the road under a sky bleeding away its sun a
car passes by on its way from somewhere gone to
an altogether other somewhere ahead and a
woman tiny and ancient behind the wheel does
not turn and she does not look at Shaw as he
struggles along the roadside with his burden.

When he veers from the road he heads not to a
fixed point but in the direction of a place removed
from the town and from the manor house both. To
the north grass thins leaving an expanse of dirt
and rock for an acre or more. He pulls the recliner
into this lot and he positions it not toward the
road and not away. A loose northwest. Here sit the
remains of a fire he's made before. He takes up the
book and he sits and opens the book to the
pamphlet's page. He reads the page and he turns a
dozen and he reads again. He makes a noise, a
pained exhale. The book lowers to his lap.

He's up and he is moving and book and
pamphlet lie in the dust at his back. He crosses
the field to the house by the road and he enters
and he searches and when he has gathered what
he seeks he returns to the chair in the clearing. He
lounges, sunk into cushions. He takes a cork from
a bottle and he sips. The sky sinks into pinks as
the sun dies away. A hawk goes on drifting

through figure eights in its graceful laze. Shaw opens a paperback novel to its first page. The cover shows a cowboy in the trappings of a western but the story is some kind of horror.

15

He kneels alongside the creek with its rolling, gurgling hum. He pulls the knife from its scabbard and digs into the dirt and he works it back and forth a dozen times, two dozen times. Worms poke from the wet ground, working their way out and coiling and flexing in their primordial pink. These unfinished organisms. Shaw plucks one and he fits it onto the curve and length of a hook attached to a line that is itself attached to the rod and reel. He lifts the rod and he stands and at the hips he turns to practice a cast and he repeats this and this time he does cast and the worm hits the water with a thump. He lays the rod across a stone and he anchors it in place with smaller stones and then he sits on a rock on which he's sat before. He watches the creek and he watches the subtle tugging on the line. He waits. In time he pulls in the line and the worm is gone. He does it all again and some hours later and some number of tries on he reels in a fish and then another. Silver things flopping. He takes each by the tail and smacks it once against the rock on which the rod is anchored. He lays the fish on a bed of grass gathered alongside the creek and goes to again cast the line. He scrapes scales away with his knife and he guts each fish the way he saw it done in a movie once years ago and he waits but in the whole of the afternoon he catches only the two.

He doesn't see the dog coming. He watches the creek and he hears the hard gallop and then the dog is there, frozen, eyes wide and mouth hard, its run ceased in an instant. It watches Shaw and Shaw sits on his rock eyeing the dog back. Its fur is a yellow gold with patches of an ashen hue, dirty, shaggy but not matted, not unwell. Seconds pass and mouth softens, falls open. Pink tongue lolls. The dog stares and it pants but it does not sit. Shaw holds up a hand.

"Hi there."

The dog's mouth clamps shut with a wet sound
and at once its respite is broken as it runs on by at
full clip. Shaw looks on at the dog's retreat and as
the line of the creek leans in a curve the dog does
vanish once more. He watches a moment longer
and he sits listening to the white noise gurgle of
the creek's eternal advance and then he is again
kneeling in the wet dirt and he is gathering grass
bed and fish and rinsing knife with a splash in the
water's flow and he's taking up rod and climbing
the ridge to the scattered trees and the open field
beyond.

The world is bruised to the north. Pillars of sun
show where rain cuts the sky. The blue above is
edging away, eaten by yards and by miles as storm
clouds draw onward. He watches, he waits. The air
is rich with that wet earth smell carried on a wind
that never ends. Shaw breathes it in over and over.
Somewhere in those far off miles a sliver of
lightning flashes in the day but the sound of its
lashing out never reaches this place.

***

The noise is constant. It is abrasive. Rain hitting
roof, hitting every surface with its crisp slap. He

tries to push closed the door but the latch is weakened by age and it blows open at once. He sits on the edge of the bed. He puts his head in his hands and squeezes and he lets go again. He shakes his head. The noise of the rain consumes all other sound.

The fish sit on the steps, uncooked, still in their bed of grass. He tells himself he will make the fire when the storm lets up but the storm will never let up. The wind is a moan through every crack and gap. Boards and braces grate at their rending. The room is shaking. The world is shaking. Each wall leans and somewhere there is the sound of things coming undone and then Shaw is standing and he is running into the rain and into the night and into the open field.

He climbs the manor house stairs in leaps. He grabs the door's knob and shoves but this does nothing. He takes a step back and gives the door a kick that does not shake door or rattle frame. He does it again with no more success than the first time. He walks the length of the porch and he comes back to the door. He stands staring. After a moment he goes to items left on the porch. He tears at the plastic wrapping pulled tight around the case of canned goods and when he gets one

loose he throws it through the nearest window.
With sleeve pulled over hand he clears glass from
the frame.

Getting in takes climbing and crawling. There
is no grace to the effort. Partway in he lets go and
falls. He lands on glass shards but he goes uncut
and unbruised. He stands but his legs shake. The
room in which he stands shows only a sliver of
lighter dark wavering ahead. Shaw moves. He goes
to that sliver and it expands onto a hall running
north to south from one end of the manor to the
other. He turns left toward a room lighter still and
at the north end of the manor he finds that light.
In a doorway he stops. The ceiling is open to night
where roof meets wall, and rain and the light of
silver moon come spilling in. There are no
furnishings or memories left behind save a portrait
on the wall opposite the cave-in. Beyond this the
room is bare. Shaw skirts rain and light, moving
along the room's border until he is face to face
with the man in the painting. Swollen canvas still
shows a figure of some regality, but time and the
world have distorted that polish, flaking paint
away to leave ridges and cracks and the warped
face of what once was. He looks for some minutes
into the face of this stranger and the storm still

goes on beyond these walls but even as the rain pours in through the compromised roof the storm cannot touch this place.

***

The pounding is almost polite. Each rap is measured, more than a knock but only just, a noise to call attention but not offend. It comes and it waits and then it comes again.

Shaw blinks and he looks around. The corner in which he is curled and wound is outside the water pooled from the wall opposite and curving in the room's middle. The knock comes again. Shaw stands and he stretches and falls back against a wall. A shoulder connects with an object there and he jumps and he turns as a ruined painting falls from its moorings to lay facedown in the dust. He stares at the back of this artifact and then he is moving and he is in the hallway, stumbling along in the direction of what he thinks is the front door and the someone waiting beyond.

Each footfall in an ancient wood floor comes with a dense thump and the groan of old nails. Doors stand open to empty rooms or they are closed shut to a mystery lacking the intrigue to be solved. Where stairs leading up once stood there is now a vacant nook and there above is a landing connected to nothing. Even old boards have been hauled away.

The foyer door stands open. Scattered window glass is spread across the floor. A sliding bolt at the front door's middle is thrown into a steel fastening attached to the frame and a more modest turnkey lock holds fast at the knob with key still protruding from its mechanism.

Shaw steps into the foyer. He steps through the broken glass and to the front door. He turns the bolt and yanks it free of its fastening and he turns the key until it gives a dull click. He pulls open the door on hinges that whine and the young couple is there, the boy, the girl. The boy holds a box from a chain pizza shop and the girl is nodding, she is smiling at Shaw. He stares, impassive.

"Uh huh?"

The girl goes on nodding as she responds.

"We wanted to see you. We wanted to talk to you. Can we come in?"

Shaw steps forward and they part. He pulls closed the door. Two steps bring him to the porch railing and there he stands. The boy and the girl follow. They boy sets down the pizza on top of the case of water. The girl speaks.

"We left you a number."

And the boy is there, he is talking too.

"We told a man about you."

Shaw turns to look at the girl and he looks away again.

"What man?"

"He knows us," says the girl. "He knows my uncle. He writes about these kinds of things."

There are seconds of silence before she offers a qualifier.

"For magazines."

"What kinds of things?"

"He wants to tell your story."

"What does that mean?"

"What?"

"I don't have a story."

"Man, come on."

Shaw looks down at his feet and he turns to look at the girl. The boy speaks up.

"We brought you a pizza."

There is again quiet. After a moment Shaw says he does not know the girl. He says he does not know the girl's uncle or his friend who writes about these things for magazines. He again tells the young couple he does not have a story and he tells them not to bring anyone to this place.

"Just don't say no," she says. "Just give it some thought, okay? We'll come back."

She bends to pick up the pizza box and she puts this in Shaw's hands and as he is looking at the logo stamped in red on white cardboard she is already turned and moving down the steps and away with the boy just behind. He watches the young couple cross the field and get in the roadster and he watches them both turn and the girl waves before they together disappear in the miles of road and then he too crosses those acres of stirring grassland to the porch of his little house by the road. Along the boards grass is strewn and in places it is piled in clumps and of the fish nothing remains. The prints of paws dipped in mud pace from end to porch end and they move in circles on the house's wood floor viewed through the front door standing open. Shaw sits on the porch step. He sets the pizza box down beside him on the porch proper. He lifts the lid and tears away a slice that droops in his hand. Cheese has cooled and grease congealed. He eats it down in such a hurry he comes close to choking.

16

It takes him some wandering to find it again. Among the trees, through twists that might once have been paths, Shaw moves in loops and snaking roam. The heir said it was somewhere south of the cabin in its open land but south of that clearing is anything, it could be anything. When he comes again upon the garden it is as before, by accident.

There among that acre of growth coiled under the fall of sun kneels a man in the dirt and weeds and trees and vines. He turns a face wrinkled with time to look at the place where Shaw stands at the garden's edge. Then he returns to his work. A minute goes by, and then another. In time the man speaks.

"Are you the one pilfering my garden?"

Shaw step to garden's edge.

"No, but I can trade you. I have plums."

This elder man waves a dismissive hand.

"I don't mind so much. There's plenty of pecans, but if you eat all my apples I'll cut off your hands."

He works there, snipping vines and setting blooms atop a towel and arranging others in a manner that shows care and understanding for the work he undertakes. Shaw watches the man work. He watches the studied approach to maintaining this wilderness. The gardener glances to see this studying. He speaks.

"You're staying in Sinclair's cabin."

Shaw shakes his head no.

"I live down by the road."

"But you were staying there."

"He's not coming back."

The gardener nods.

"Good. They're pirates. Those people, every one of them. The Sinclairs are pirates from all the way back."

And.

"I think he stole my chicken."

Shaw makes a noise like a word and he takes a step into the twine. He bends and takes up a pecan and another and another. He fills pockets with all they will hold and still the forest floor is saturated with hickory nuts. He looks up. The gardener is watching. He points some kind of curved scissor at different vines and roots.

"Carrots, onions."

Shaw says okay. He says he'll come back and he thanks the gardener. The gardener is nodding and he holds up a hand and then he walks off a few paces into the denser growth. When he returns he has a yellow apple in hand. He passes this over to Shaw and Shaw gives his thanks again. He hesitates. Then he asks.

"Have you seen a dog?"

"Sure," says the gardener. "Everybody has."

***

He stares across the field with apple in hand. His bite is noisy, that crisp rending. When he wades out into the grass he still chews and he swallows and takes another bite and another and when there is only core left he tosses this away where it vanishes forever among the billowing hay.

108

At the steps and up. The door opens with ease now. The manor house entryway yawns in wide gape, a cave leading down to the past. When Shaw steps into the foyer he turns to where key protrudes from lock and he takes this and slips it into a pants pocket.

He stops just beyond the foyer. A line of shoeprints in the dust run the length of the hall and another returns where before he came and went. Nothing is changed in this place. He steps into that dust again, and where doors stand open he looks in, he looks around, and where he finds them closed he turns knobs and pushes in, and some need a shove, and some need a lift or a kick or a determined, focused shake, but each room does give away its secrets in time. Each room holds nothing save that wounded suite, that makeshift sunroom. Here Shaw enters, and where the portrait lay still facedown he does stop. A nail lies in the dust where it has fallen. Shaw nudges it with a toe. That rusted barb rolls in a circle and stops. Shaw takes a pecan from his left coat pocket and with a hand he presses its shell against the wall until there is a crack. He peels meat from shell and eats a little at a time, and when he has emptied that husk he takes shell pieces and slips them into the pocket opposite. Then he returns to the hall.

Where once stairs climbed up to the second-story landing there is only wall. Shaw stands staring beneath that open ledge. He eats another pecan and deposits the shell as before. He looks at the wall and the floor and the ledge again. He backs away and stands on toes to look at the walkway above but he sees no more than before. Then he is turning and walking down hall and out through the front door.

When Shaw returns he holds a heavy stone cupped in a palm and tucked under an arm he carries a load of planks dragged from among the ruins. He creaks his way along boards. At the place where once stairs stood he takes rock and old nails and knocks a dried slat in place on bare wall. Above it he drives in another. He does this up and up until a crude ladder forms. That oval of stone hammers nail as it may but joints cramp and fingers bruise and the work is slow going in its antediluvian fervor.

He climbs. Rungs wobble but hold under his ascent. He makes the second floor landing with first a hand and then another and he throws his weight up and over with a heave that knocks the wind from his gut. He rolls over and lies in the dust. When he breathes again he sucks in air in great gulps and waits. In time he stands.

He does it all again, going up halls and back down, opening doors, leaning into rooms or stepping into rooms and checking corners, checking closets. Each second-story room is as empty as below save one, which must have been an office once. A rolltop desk sits under a fall of dust and years and of its once varied instruments of pens and writings and the baubles of personality there are none remaining but a simple and ancient rotary phone. Shaw takes up the handset and turns it in his hand. He puts it to his ear and then he looks at it again. He sets it back in its cradle and he picks up base and handset both. Underneath is a square of clear wood where no dust has yet fallen. He turns back to the doorway and to the hall beyond. He holds the phone to him. The weight of the thing. Its frame is black metal that carries a heft it does not show. He turns back to the desk and sets the base back in its square of cleared desk and this done he leaves this room.

Down the ladder. The stone hammer waits on the floor where it was dropped. Shaw takes the

stone and moves up the hall to the open chamber
with its fallen ceiling. The light through that
exposed wound is bruised and fading. There on
the floor sits the portrait, the nail. He takes up nail
and knocks it three times, four times, enough to
sink it back into the hole from which it slipped.
When that spike holds fast he bends and retrieves
the old wooden frame and with some care hooks
the latch affixed to its back onto that rusted peg.
Paint has flaked in the falling and the face there is
all the more warped, obscured, the delicate
features that survived these years now lost for
good.

Shaw dusts his hands on pants. He stands
looking at the portrait for some time. He looks at
the floor around him as if there might be
something to be done but there is not. When he
leaves there is still sun showing through the
collapsed roof but it is a weak and feeble thing, a
thing not long for this world. He crosses one last
time through that stretched length of hall and at
the foyer doorway he turns and looks once more.
In the dust show tracks of countless feet coming
and going, wandering, violating this mausoleum.
Undertaking some unnamed taboo. Shaw moves
out through the foyer.

Outside the front door he takes key from
pocket and pushes it into the works and turns
until the mechanism utters a satisfying click. He
takes the key again and steps to the shattered
window and with a toss the key goes clanking into
the dark within.

***

He returns to his little house by the road before
the last of the sun is gone from the world. He sits
on steps and he looks out at the trees now only an
outline, a shape in the dark unbroken by
definition or detail. He shatters pecan's shell on
the boards of the porch and he chews the meat in
unhurried devouring.

Distant headlights pierce the night running
north and in minutes they pass and sometime later
a second set follows the first. Off to the north
another set appears but their approach is a
crawling thing and by the time they come upon
Shaw's town the last of day has gone. A tractor. As
it nears a light comes on in the cab and the
woman directing this behemoth offers up the
same wave she's thrown to Shaw in days past. He
waves back from his place in the fall of her light.

Then the tractor is past and it is pulling off onto gravel roadside and the woman in the cab is leaning down out of sight and she is gone for seconds. When she comes up the light goes out.

The tractor rumbles in low idle. A shape moves in the dark and when it nears it coalesces and it is the woman and she is holding out a bottle by the neck for Shaw to take. He does accept this offering and the glass is sweating and it is cool in his hand. She takes a seat next to him on the steps. He pulls at the bottle cap but the top is not a screw. He takes a green plastic lighter from a pocket and wedges open the bottle. The cap clinks in the dark. She reaches for the lighter and wedges open her own bottle and she hands the lighter back. They sip and the bottles hold cheap American beer and Shaw says thank you. He asks her what she does and she says to him she is a rancher and a reaper and a breeder. She does not ask Shaw what he does. They talk and sip. She is some years his senior. The night sounds fade and conversation wanders where it might as they go on discussing nothing of any real importance.

17

He lays out his gear in meticulous preparation alongside the creek; rod, knife, grass bed. He takes up his knife and farms for worms and he is doing this still when he hears what might be a voice far off, a vague hallooing. Shaw lays down his knife. He sits listening. The creek gurgles and whispers and the trees shiver and after a moment the voice comes again, distant and indistinct. He rises and crosses the creek and climbs the ridge. He stops to listen but the world is quiet. He moves through the field with its scrub and past the plum tree and on. Ahead the land drops and it becomes impossibly flat and a sea of high grasses sloshes and sways. Signs rise from the current to warn of trespass and danger and other things too faded to read. And in that churning sea there does sit a machine in its slow rusting, a block the size of a truck with parts rotting and a rusted cone the length of a car, a drill once. Farther along there sits decomposing a sedan of some luxury from long ago. Shaw follows the land's descent and he wades into that plain.

The car. Soft angles and swoops in old steel hide among the rot. A door has been stripped away and lost. Shaw puts a hand on the roof and eases onto a seat of pulled foam and springs among old leather and dead grass. Fingers grip a wheel smooth and thin. Eyes close and the land is not this land but another, and these flowing fields are miles of pavement or they are lots on left and right cut by a road leading between distinct worlds, or they are a landscape barren after some nightmare machine has quarried and dozed clean the globe to leave behind this flat earth.

Shaw leans back. He opens his eyes. From a pocket he pulls a cigarette pack and a lighter and from the pack he shakes free a bent cigarette. He puts it in his mouth and he lights it and after he inhales smoke leaks in fine trails from mouth and nose. He looks out at the world before his car, at the grassland there waving in tender breath of air.

In the distance beyond the plain there rises a
mound of grass with sharp sides like some
primordial pyramid lost to time and beyond this
there is nothing. There is nothing.

***

He fishes enough to catch only one. The sun is
falling away when he goes to make a fire atop the
ash of fires that have come before. He puts a
match to gathered scrub and cups the heat and
blows a gentle breath. A car passes on the road
but Shaw does not look away from the fire. It
catches and spreads and soon old wood is popping
under a bed of flame. With a foot he shoves a rock
long and flat into the fire's middle. He waits. He
sits in the recliner and watches the flames dance
and move. Shadow draws as near it can as the last
of day passes. When enough time has gone by
Shaw uses a stick to draw back the rock. He lays
the fish on the rock where it sizzles and cooks and
he turns it over with his knife and a careful hand
and does it all again. He sips water from a glass jar
and he pours a little on the rock to produce a hiss
that for a moment stills the night. He eats the fish
with fingers that drip with grease and he eats a

plum in much the same fashion and when this is done he leans back into cushions rich with an odorous must and breathes in the night. Fire crackles and nips and the things that move in the grass chirrup and they sing and grouse and Shaw listens and he waits for a voice to speak or a figure to move near but the things outside the touch of fire's light do still remain so.

18

It's one in a series, the book in his hand. It is a western, a story of ungovernable men and their quests and their conflicts. Guns and grit and drama and doom. He turns pages under an afternoon sun and the futility of these men and their choices plays out the way it always does.

On the road there is a truck, a long trailer parked off where the land trails away. Men move about but they are lines on the horizon and their movements are indistinct twirlings. In time a mower breaks away from their doings and another just like it moves along the road's opposite shoulder. Each machine moves in a line up the road for a distance before circling back once and then repeating this trek before moving on to the next length of acreage.

Shaw looks up from his book now and then to watch the approach of the mowers and he does this still as they grow smaller in the distance to the north. In time they are followed by men with an instrument they stick into the ground and lean to look at or look through, and sometimes they stop to talk, and sometimes they leave behind a tiny orange flag in the cleared away roadside. The workers move on their way and another truck comes along, a pickup now with more equipment that is set up and arranged and broken down again with the specifics of its every act remaining at best a mystery. Sometime later these men too disappear in the distance.

Shaw reads his book. He reads as afternoon hours fall by and he is reading still as under a sky of pinks and spilled purples there comes the far-off roar of a monster's engine. He puts a finger in his book to mark the page. On the road passes a phantom, a wraith, an ancient muscle car that has screamed by on these miles of road again and again and again. Shaw watches. He watches its approach from his first hearing and until it has faded away altogether he does not look away. And still he looks out at the road as if that phantom might again at any moment appear. When a minute has gone by and the road remains empty he opens the book and his eyes again find the page.

He does not see the dog emerge from the grass. He takes a glance up from the story he holds and there it sits, not close but it is there in the clearing, sitting, looking at Shaw. Shaw taps his knee and he calls to the dog but the dog only watches.

"Yeah, well."

He turns again to his book and is lost in the words there when his eye catches the movement of the dog coming near. It comes and again sits and at the foot of the recliner molding in this anywhere field that dog lays down and in seconds breathes the deep heaving of sleep.

Shaw leans and he looks at the dog where it lay. He reaches out a hand and there he stops. He doesn't pet the dog, he doesn't touch it.

"Good. Okay."

He watches the dog stir and still and breathe those long draws of air. On his face is a smile he does not know is coming before it is there. He sits back with his book.

On the road the men have returned. The workers in their pickup. Voices carry across the land, talking, laughing. They sit in the truck bed under the last dregs of day and they drink from bottles and they laugh. Their work is not ended, their work does not end, but they have in this moment in this place the only respite that comes.

Shaw wakes to a sky of stars. So many stars. The dog is gone and the workers are gone and he is alone in this place. He closes his eyes and he swallows. He reaches for the fading remains of a dream but the only detail left is the roar given off by that old muscle car.

19

He considers ignoring them. For a minute he does. For more than a minute he thinks he will ignore them. Then he is getting up and running out onto the porch and around the little house and into the field and he is calling to them long before they reach the manor house. The young couple. They stop and they turn as Shaw catches up to where they stand waiting.

"We got you a motel."

It's the first thing she says. Shaw stops and the girl steps closer and she says it again.

"Just for today. We got you a room. It's all set up. The journalist is in the next room."

"The journalist."

"The guy. You talk. Stay the night. See what you think. Tomorrow we bring you back. That's the deal."

"And then you'll go."

"Well. If he sells you on it. I mean. If you want him to tell your story you'll need to talk. More. A lot more."

"But if I don't?"

"Well just come talk."

Shaw says he needs to get his coat. He turns and he heads back to the house by the road and he does not see the look shared between the young couple, a pause. He grabs his coat in the little room and he does a turn as if he is forgetting something but there is nothing here to forget and he again steps out the door. He pulls the door closed but the latch doesn't hold and with a foot he slides over a rock kept for this purpose. He shifts the rock into place and again pulls shut the door and this time it does stay, wedged just so atop the rock.

The young couple wait at the car. The girl opens a door and the boy opens a door and Shaw heads for the near side, the passenger. The boy moves the seat and Shaw climbs in back and then the couple are in and the car is moving.

The whir of tire on road is the only sound for minutes. Shaw looks out the window at passing miles of that same swaying grass. When the boy asks about the radio Shaw goes on looking at the world going by. He says anything is fine. The boy says something to the girl and she says something back and Shaw hears none of this and then a song is playing, a new voice singing lyrics decades old.

At the town's edge they pass a gas station. They pass a football field with wooden bleachers and rusted goalposts and they pass another gas station, other structures with no signs at all. Beyond this is what might have once been a set of offices. Modern architecture in faded blues and whites. Every window broken. They drive on by.

Downtown is made up of storefronts, a diner, a bar, a shop selling the legs of frogs. Some roads are lined with old brick. The ride yields a satisfying murmur as these throwbacks are traversed.

The motel is a line of apartments. It is a single-building two-story row of hovels painted seventies red. The roadster pulls to a stop in a faded space next to a room with a sign saying OFFICE. The girl gets out and the boy gets out and they move to the door and in.

Shaw steps out of the car. He looks to the room the young couple entered but he does not follow. The door hangs open by only a crack. He waits. On the street a sedan passes with the rise and fall of a pop song spilling from open window. Shaw closes his eyes and tries to place the song but he cannot.

And the couple is there, and they have a key, they are ushering Shaw to a room with a number matching that stamped into the key fob. The girl opens the door and she turns on the light to a room drab but functional. End table, cheap chairs. Paisley coverlet sheaths a single bed. Clothes are laid out, black slacks, white shirt, socks, boxers. Neat, each article beside the next.

"We took a guess at the sizes."

The boy is outside. He is knocking on another door and then he is speaking with someone there. When the boy enters the motel room he is followed by an older man in a tailored shirt of some fine make and a black hooded sweatshirt. The trousers the man wears are showy dress pants but wrinkled. His shoes are sneakers. The hand he offers has the fine bones of a bird. Shaw takes the man's hand and gives a brief shake. The girl introduces him as the journalist and no one gives

him another name. An awkward back and forth
ensues and Shaw ignores their banter and then
the couple is leaving and the journalist is leaving
and when the door is closed Shaw finds himself
alone.

Concrete separating first floor from second
reverberates with strange lives, thuds and scrapes
and wordless talk. Shaw steps into a bathroom
painted an unwell yellow and he pulls aside a
shower curtain decorated with cartoon daisies. He
turns a knob and cold water sprays. He steps back.
He does a circuit of the main room as shower
drowns out some of the cacophony. He throws
filthy clothes on the bed and showers in white
noise quiet and when once again he stands wet in
the midst of that clanging affront he pulls on each
article of his unwashed garb.

The roadster is gone from the lot. Shaw moves
past the sparse accumulation of cars there and
down the block until he comes again to the shops
and storefronts that make up downtown. On the
other side of a window is a diner full of tables
occupied by mothers and fathers and children
talking and eating and laughing under lights warm
and inviting. The bar next door is much the same,
the lighting, the patrons. Shaw keeps walking.

The edge of town is not far. There among the gas stations and detritus is a wooden building nailed together a century ago or more and when Shaw opens its door cool lighting and cigarette smoke comes pouring out. He enters and he sits. A few tables house men drinking alone and at the bar sit only Shaw and another man. The journalist.

"There he is."

The journalist's voice is filled with honest mirth. Shaw nods but does not respond. He waves over a pale boy tending bar. He asks the bartender if they have a kitchen and the bartender says they do.

"You make burgers?"

"Yeah."

"Can I get it undercooked?"

"How undercooked?"

"What's the one that's more red than pink?"

"Rare?"

"Rare, then."

"They won't let us sell it like that."

The bartender says it in a voice clear but bored and when he repeats the request to a man in the kitchen he orders the burger rare. Then he is back and he's pouring for the journalist and when the

journalist says another for my friend the bartender
is pouring one for Shaw too. Shaw sniffs at the
glass and the oily fluid there smells like butter. He
drinks his drink and he thanks the journalist and
then his meal arrives. Burger and fries on paper
plate doubled up to soak grease. He bites and
burger wells with juices, some blood, some fat.

The journalist is talking, he is saying he's gonna
buy Shaw another drink, he's gonna ask him a few
questions, that's it. He says if it gives him
something to think about maybe he'll have a story
to tell. Shaw talks and the journalist talks and the
things the journalist says are more statements than
questions. He orders drinks from a bottle with a
moon on its label and he laughs at things he
himself says. Then it is done, he is thanking Shaw
for his time and it is done.

"That's it?"

The journalist shrugs. His eyes fall closed when
he does.

"Think so. I'm gonna think on it. Gonna go to
my room and drink after I finish drinking and I'm
gonna think on it."

Shaw says okay. He pulls bills from his coat
pocket and lays two on the bar. He sets his empty
glass atop this and the journalist is watching. Then

Shaw is turning and he is walking away and out and the journalist watches this too.

The sun is gone but the night holds onto its heat. Shaw walks along a road with no sidewalks until he comes to a gas station leaking white light from every window. A bell rings at his entry and here he walks among rows of items he has seen in every store in every city and town. A song plays, one he has heard but does not know. He looks at goods arranged on shelves but he is not seeing these. There is a detached feeling that begins to set in. He thinks he is dizzy but this isn't it. When he gets to the counter he is sweating.

"Where's your liquor?"

The clerk has a wild smile, this child. He has eyes too wide, showing too much white. He says this is a dry county. He says restaurants, bars, that's where you'll find your drink. He says there's beer here. He points to the coolers at the room's other end.

Shaw offers no response at all before moving back into night. There is a breeze that takes the edge off the heat just a bit but not enough. He thinks he might take off his coat but he does not. He walks. When he finds himself back at the bar he goes in.

The journalist is leaned down and forward and he is staring at the wall behind the bar. When Shaw steps near the journalist turns and he speaks.

"Look at you."

"You have a bottle in your room?"

"I do."

"You think of any more questions?"

"Hell, I don't know."

The journalist drinks what is left in his glass.

"Pay the bill," he says.

***

The journalist's room is identical to Shaw's. A messenger bag and a duffel bag sit tossed on the floor. The television is on but the sound is turned low. On the screen an infomercial plays. An ad for some kind of pan. The journalist sits in a cheap plastic chair and Shaw sits in another and each man holds a small paper cup. On the floor between the two men there is a bottle. The cheapest whiskey. There is talk, and some of the talk is questions and some is storytelling and some is men rambling. They drink and refill their paper cups and they drink again. When the journalist

says to start at the beginning Shaw tells him he
was going to lose his house. He says he couldn't
win so he opted to escape.

"Escape."

"Yes."

"Let me tell you about escape."

The journalist pauses. He sits forward and
reaches down between his knees for the bottle on
the floor. He yanks the cork with a pop and pours
until half the cup is darkened with this rotgut
swill. He sips and sips again. When he speaks
again he says people leave the Old World for the
New. They leave the Settled East for the Wild
West. Always people want to escape. They want
the option. Always they will. But there is no New
World anymore. There's no Wild West.

Shaw looks at the journalist. He watches the
man as he talks and he watches him still when he
has quieted. He does not believe the things the
journalist says and he doesn't believe the
journalist believes them. Some time goes by in the
quiet. Then Shaw speaks.

"I keep seeing a car."

"What's that?"

"On the road."

"Well. That's where cars go."

Shaw looks away. The journalist exhales a deep huff.

"Okay. Tell me about the car."

Shaw begins to talk but his description is vague and when he has given out the details he begins again with the same recitation. Muscle car. Old. So loud. A phantom.

"Is it real?"

"It's a car. A real car."

"Man, I don't know you. I'm asking."

Shaw tells the journalist he first saw it the night he left the city. He says he spoke with a man who was hitchhiking and later he saw that man as a passenger in that car, and he saw it again the next morning with only the driver inside.

"So the passenger got where he was going."

Shaw shakes his head but he doesn't give voice to what this might mean. The journalist is nodding. He's saying this is good. He is saying I can work with this.

From there they talk more, they drink more. From there the night becomes flashes. It becomes moments. Shaw urinating in a parking lot under humming, pale lights. A stranger yelling and another laughing. Glass breaking. A car's engine roaring and then slowly dying away.

20

He can ignore the knocking. It is a thing without consequence existing somewhere on the outside of his sleep. When they ring his room he sleeps through that too. He turns over and he pulls at a sheet but he never surfaces from a sleep that is full, that is encompassing.

Some hours later he sits up. His pulse is heavy in his ears. Heart pounding. When he opens his eyes the colors of the world are too sharp, too bright. He throws his legs over the side of the bed and gets to his feet and there he just stands. He looks down at himself and runs hands down his wrinkled, unwashed clothes. He straightens his belt and sits back on the bed to pull on socks, shoes. He goes on sitting for another minute before he pulls on his coat.

The sun overhead casts the world in pale glow. He squints as he crosses the street to the diner there. He takes a table near a waitress with the ovoid skull of a doll. She smiles with every inch of her face as she takes his order. Beans, rice, tamales. Mexican food, Mexican beer. He says he's supposed to meet a man here and the waitress says that man's come and gone. She tells Shaw where that man can be found.

When his food comes he eats each bite with slow care. Every forkful is chased with a drink to wash it down. Halfway through the plate he needs a second beer.

He doesn't speak to the young couple when they come in. They take their own booth by the door and they make their order with the same smiling waitress. She smiles again at Shaw as she goes to deliver the young couple's order to the kitchen.

When Shaw's plate is clean and he's wiping his mouth and hands with a fat wad of napkins the young couple's girl chooses then to step near.

"We came by. We looked for you."

Shaw tells the girl he slept in. He says he was out late with the journalist. Her mouth spreads in delight. She glows, she beams.

"Where is he?"

"I'm meeting him at the bar."

"Next door?"

Shaw says no. He says it's the bar at the edge of town.

"Oh. The knife fight bar."

"Well."

Shaw sits in unnatural silence a moment. Then he is pulling cash from his pocket and laying out bills, more than enough, double enough. He lays an unused table knife lengthwise across the layered bills and returns the rest to the pocket of his coat and he stands and he does not make eye contact as the girl begins to laugh at what she has just seen.

***

"There he is."

The journalist raises a glass as Shaw enters the bar. Shaw orders a drink and the journalist empties his glass and says he'll have one too. He asks Shaw questions and his questions are much the same as the night prior and the answers Shaw gives are much the same too. The young couple are not there and then they are and they listen and they drink and then they drink more. Afternoon becomes evening and evening becomes night and it goes on, the drinking, the talking. The journalist is in conversation with the bartender and the young couple are in conversation with each other and Shaw watches these things from the end of the bar. Their words come in bursts among bar noise static, indecipherable transmissions there in the fog. A man is standing near the girl, a stranger in a working man's suit, fabric thick and loose. He speaks and the girl turns to him and what he said he says again. The girl laughs and he leans down so that his eyes are square with hers, and what he says now is heard by her alone. Then her hand flashes out and swings and in it is a bowl or an ashtray molded in heavy glass and when it connects with the stranger's temple there comes a hideous thump and as that man drops violence does come, and there is shouting, and there is worse. Shaw drinks down his drink and he drinks another off the bar and then he is backing away from a series of choices that all will find they regret.

And he is gone, and their fates and their choices are again behind him. He walks along the road until the town is at his back like some

dilapidated outpost at the edge of the world. He
does not stop, he does not look back. He walks for
hours in the night and in all that time no car
comes along, no horns or songs, no voices. Only
footsteps and the sigh of trees.

It is any hour when he arrives at the little house
by the road. He goes in and he shuts the door but
the wind at once pushes it open again. He stands
in the endless black and strips off his coat and
throws it where he thinks the bed lies there in the
dark. He closes his eyes and opens them but no
more of the world resolves. And the sound is
there, the roar, that phantom still some miles off.
He wants to move but he does not. He waits there
in the dark. When it does not go on by he is
unsurprised. When the engine shuts off there in
the road still he waits. That old muscle car engine
ticking. The door cries out with the fierce wail of
some ancient banshee, and a boot steps out onto
roadside gravel, and another, and they walk, they
round that stilled phantom and move up the steps
and nearer the door standing open, and the figure
there stops, staring into a darkness where Shaw
stands, not moving, not breathing, not knowing if
he is seen at all.

Craig Rodgers is the author of stories that have appeared in *Juked*, *Heart of Farkness*, *Clash Media*, *Not One of Us*, and others. He spends most of his time writing in North Texas.